• THE SOCRATIC METHOD •

"Maybe Julian wasn't—I mean, maybe the restaurant made an honest mistake."

"What do you know about hemlock, Miss Jansson?"

"Socrates drank some."

"That was from a tree—yew tree," said Homicide Lieutenant Surgelato. "This is a weed—like a big carrot plant. A cubic inch of the root will kill you after three or four hours. Malaise but no nausea. But you took botany at Stanford. I don't have to tell *you* this. Point is, you gotta go *find* hemlock. Disturbed ground near wetlands or woods. You don't just pick it up at the supermarket."

A shoulder-padded man laid a smooth white hand on my arm. "Long time! Great suit!" When I didn't reply, he persisted, "Don't you recognize me?"

Aaron Bancroft, who'd once led thousands of us in a march on Washington, now handed me his business card: *Consultant, the Elliot wave theory of stock market fluctuation*. Luckily he spotted some other acquaintances, and flitted off to give *them* his card.

"*Networking* at a funeral!"

"He's more useful to society this way than throwing Molotov cocktails at banks," Surgelato muttered.

I grinned. "Julian got him acquitted of that charge."

A WILLA JANSSON MYSTERY

Bantam Books offers the finest in classic and modern American murder mysteries. Ask your bookseller for the books you have missed.

Stuart Palmer
THE PENGUIN POOL MURDER
THE PUZZLE OF THE HAPPY
  HOOLIGAN
THE PUZZLE OF THE RED STALLION
THE PUZZLE OF THE SILVER
  PERSIAN

Craig Rice
THE LUCKY STIFF

Rex Stout
BROKEN VASE
DEATH OF A DUDE
DEATH TIMES THREE
FER-DE-LANCE
THE FINAL DEDUCTION
GAMBIT
THE RUBBER BAND

Max Allan Collins
THE DARK CITY

William Kienzle
THE ROSARY MURDERS

Joseph Louis
MADELAINE
STEPHANIE

M. J. Adamson
NOT TIL A HOT JANUARY
A FEBRUARY FACE
REMEMBER MARCH

Conrad Haynes
BISHOP'S GAMBIT, DECLINED

Barbara Paul
FIRST GRAVEDIGGER
THE FOURTH WALL
KILL FEE
THE RENEWABLE VIRGIN
BUT HE WAS ALREADY DEAD WHEN
  I GOT THERE

P. M. Carlson
MURDER UNRENOVATED

Ross Macdonald
THE GOODBYE LOOK
SLEEPING BEAUTY
THE NAME IS ARCHER
THE DROWNING POOL
THE UNDERGROUND MAN

Margaret Maron
THE RIGHT JACK

William Murray
WHEN THE FAT MAN SINGS

Keith Peterson
THE TRAPDOOR

Robert Goldsborough
MURDER IN E MINOR
DEATH ON DEADLINE

Sue Grafton
"A" IS FOR ALIBI
"B" IS FOR BURGLAR
"C" IS FOR CORPSE

R. D. Brown
HAZZARD
VILLA HEAD

A. E. Maxwell
JUST ANOTHER DAY IN PARADISE
THE FROG AND THE SCORPION

Rob Kantner
BACK-DOOR MAN
THE HARDER THEY HIT

Joseph Telushkin
THE UNORTHODOX MURDER OF
  RABBI WAHL

Richard Hilary
SNAKE IN THE GRASSES
PIECES OF CREAM

Carolyn G. Hart

DESIGN FOR MURDER
DEATH ON DEMAND

Lia Matera
WHERE LAWYERS FEAR TO TREAD
A RADICAL DEPARTURE

Robert Crais
THE MONKEY'S RAINCOAT

A RADICAL DEPARTURE

•

Lia Matera

BANTAM BOOKS
TORONTO • NEW YORK • LONDON • SYDNEY • AUCKLAND

The characters, law firms, and union locals depicted in this novel are imaginary. Any resemblance they bear to actual people or institutions is coincidental.

A RADICAL DEPARTURE
A Bantam Book / March 1988

Grateful acknowledgment is made for permission to reprint lyrics from "Green Green Grass of Home," by Curly Putman, copyright © 1965 Tree Publishing Co. All rights reserved. Used by permission.

ISBN 0-553-27072-9

Published simultaneously in the United States and Canada

Bantam Books are published by Bantam Books, a division of Bantam Doubleday Dell Publishing Group, Inc. Its trademark, consisting of the words "Bantam Books" and the portrayal of a rooster, is Registered in U.S. Patent and Trademark Office and in other countries. Marca Registrada. Bantam Books, 666 Fifth Avenue, New York, New York 10103.

PRINTED IN THE UNITED STATES OF AMERICA
KR   0 9 8 7 6 5 4 3 2 1

*To Peter—for leaving the job of his
(politically correct) dreams,
and moving back to the seashore.*

• CHAPTER ONE •

Julian Warneke rubbed the rim of his demitasse cup with a sliver of orange rind. The law partners on either side of him followed his decorous example. We were in a pink-tablecloth, silver-wine-bucket kind of restaurant called René's; the sort of place that serves sorbet between courses "to cleanse the palate." I assumed the orange-rind manuever was another sop to the pretentious palate. If Julian had stuck a crucifix into his amaretto mousse and eaten it with his necktie I'd have accepted it without batting an eye, so pronounced was his air of savoir faire.

Julian Warneke was a white-haired man with a disparaging mouth, a nose that curved like a small banana, and creamy, unlined skin that sagged around the eyes and at the jowls. He always looked crisp and unhurried, and he was ludicrously punctilious toward our two secretaries, while working me and the low-ranking law partners like serfs.

Julian had been famous since 1963, when a racist southern judge had jailed him for bringing a lawsuit to desegregate public schools in Mississippi. Since then he'd shifted gradually from criminal defense of Yippies, draft resisters, and Black Panthers to copyright protection of their memoirs, fitness books, and meditations on Jesus.

I worked for Julian. I did the dull bread-and-butter lawyering—the divorces, the landlord-tenant and drunk-driving defenses. The partners in the law firm—one a radical

1

investment counselor ("Don't invest in apartheid"), one a revered labor lawyer with a stereotypically cigar-chomping clientele, and another who spent most of his time entertaining Democratic assemblymen at his Napa Valley vineyard— weren't about to give the new girl their interesting cases: they weren't all *that* liberal.

Not that I was complaining. The credentialed lefties of Warneke, Kerry, Lieberman & Flish had doubtless been on the prowl for a black, Spanish-speaking Navajo woman from Vietnam. Under ordinary circumstances, they'd have been reluctant to hire a (seemingly) cutesy little blonde. But my parents had been walking Clement Kerrey's picket lines and baking banana breads for Julian Warneke's incarcerated clients for over fifteen years.

When I told my mother I'd never have gotten the job without "connections," she nearly swooned with indignation.

"Willa! How can you say that! When you did so well in law school! Editor of your law review!" My mother had a veiny foot in the kitchen sink; she was rinsing it after a Walk for Hunger. "Not that Julian is *accomplishment* oriented, when so few young people have the opportunity to develop their—"

"Mother, Julian won't interview anyone who isn't in the top ten percent of a law school class. I've never heard him speculate that maybe the other ninety percent didn't have the opportunity—"

"Well, but Baby, he needs the *very best* lawyers to defend the unfortunate and underprivileged—"

"Aaron Bancroft"—once a famous young anarchist—"is getting a hundred grand to do a videocassette about *networking*! Julian just negotiated the contract."

My mother frowned at a knobby and inflamed toe. "Aaron was such a good speaker; it's too bad." She crossed herself. This was a habit she'd acquired of late, when speaking of fallen liberals (it was too late to save the souls of conservatives, presumably).

"Julian pays his lawyers less than almost any other firm in town, did you know that?"

"But maybe that's because—"

"—he can get away with it, which is exactly why any capitalist—"

"—so much of his work is pro bono. Your father and I only paid what we could afford when we—"

"Mother! I worked two jobs so you could pay off Julian after you smashed the nose cone of that missile!"

"But you shouldn't have! We'd have been *happy* to go with the Weillars and—"

"Oh, great! Rob a bank for peace!"

She slid her foot out of the sink and let it drop to the floor, rubbing her hip. "That reminds me, I should bake them a banana bread before visiting day." Unhunched, she looked slimmer than most women her age, though she was decidedly pear shaped and rearranged by gravity. She pushed flyaway yellow-gray hair off her face.

"Anyway, Julian could certainly afford to pay me a living wage! Our 'working lunches' must cost five hundred bucks a pop!"

Which is why I now felt a trifle irritated watching Julian moisten the rim of his demitasse with a curlicue of orange rind.

No casual observer would have guessed any of us were Democrats, much less out-of-the-closet socialists.

On the other hand, I'd just spent a month in Lawton, Oklahoma, and I was glad to be back in civilization, if you can call San Francisco civilized. After a twenty-six-day argument with someone whose politics dated back to the sweatshop era of rampaging capitalism, it felt good to be comfortably surrounded by compromised lefties again. And if my lunch was inappropriately expensive, well, at least *I* wasn't paying for it, not directly anyway, and the cannoli was terrific. (Oklahoma's idea of a foreign food is Straw Hat Pizza.)

So when Julian Warneke began offering me advice about a jury trial I was preparing, I ate my cannoli and refrained from telling him that he was full of sorbet. Julian's trial technique favored political grandstanding over stick-to-the-point argument, which is fine if your client appreciates guerrilla theater and likes prison food.

The waiter came with more coffee, recognized Clement Kerrey as his union's lawyer, and launched into a bitter diatribe about his boss.

Clement dabbed his tidy gray beard with a linen napkin. "Your union has a grievance procedure," he observed coolly. Clement represented unions, not employees.

The waiter grew redder of face, muttered a few unkind words about his union, and hinted darkly that the waiters wanted to strike.

Clement Kerrey, an emaciated and reserved man with glittery black eyes, was clearly alarmed—God forbid they should picket his favorite restaurant.

Julian cut in with a peremptory, "Check, please."

The waiter correctly interpreted this as a dismissal; he stalked off, leaving me holding out my empty coffee cup.

Brian Lieberman leaned forward, glanced over his shoulder, and said confidentially, "That reminds me, we should decide about Mae."

Brian was the quintessentially San Franciscan male. As natty as any gay man (though he made a point of his heterosexuality), he always looked freshly shaved and massaged, and his dimpled face was as golden as a Napa Valley apricot. He could tell you sad stories about how great a given restaurant had been before it had been—horrors!—discovered; he could tell you the *real* reason the symphony had let its conductor go; he could tell you where to find the cheapest Bimmer on the peninsula.

Clement Kerrey shook his head sadly. "We'll have to let Mae go."

"What?" I choked on the dregs of my coffee. "Are you talking about Mae Siegel?"

Mae was one of the firm's two secretaries. I "shared" her with Felix Flish. Felix, the firm's computer whiz and de facto office manager, was constantly foisting new software on Mae, so she rarely had time to do anything except curse at her terminal. The other secretary, Maria, ended up doing most of my work.

Felix, a very tall man with a thin, horsey face and a big, bridgeless nose, assumed an upper-crusty British accent. "We cahn't have the hired help behaving sluttishly."

Clement stiffened, shifting his weight to allow the waiter to offer the check to Julian for his signature. "Not at all. You know we love Mae. It's a matter of—"

Julian cut in deftly. "We'll shelve this till the partners' meeting, I think." He frowned at the check, calculated an inflated tip, and signed for the lunch.

Felix, slouching sloppily between Julian and Brian, smiled at me. Of the firm's five attorneys, only I was not yet a partner.

Apparently Julian thought I'd come down on the side of sluttishness in the workplace.

I never got a chance to find out what he thought. Julian fished the garnish out of his half-eaten mousse, something he invariably did. The garnish looked like a piece of glazed apple or pear, cut into a rosette. I glanced at Julian as he popped it into his mouth; he made a face as if it were bitter, but he was too polite to spit the thing out.

By evening, the grand old man of left-wing politics was in the hospital with hemlock poisoning, the restaurant was swearing it didn't garnish its desserts with poisonous roots, the police were knocking at my apartment door with a search warrant, and reporters were chortling with glee to discover I'd been a suspect in the so-called "law school murders" two years earlier.

• CHAPTER TWO •

"**I**sn't it kind of tacky for you to be at the funeral?"

"Standard operating procedure," Homicide Lieutenant Don Surgelato informed me. "I'm not questioning anyone, Miss Jansson, just observing."

I checked the top buttons of my blouse, as that seemed to be what he was observing. "You're questioning *me*."

Don Surgelato used to be some kind of football star, and he'd retained a penchant for the dumb jock look—tight suit, shirt collar too loose, tie badly knotted. To complete the picture, he had a naturally stubborn expression, a low-hanging, face-traversing brow, and a Big Man smile, which he now displayed for me. "Not questioning. Besides, we're old friends."

Old friends. Over a six-month period, Surgelato had repeatedly interrogated me about the murders of my fellow law-review editors. That was two years ago—and I hadn't missed him.

"Gee—sorry I forgot your birthday, Lieutenant." I stepped aside to let a group of Teamsters with Elvis Presley haircuts into the "chapel."

We were on one of San Francisco's windiest corners, on a street that roared with traffic, outside a wood-floored funeral parlor that had recently been a Ukrainian lodge and still smelled faintly of piroshkis. The place lacked elegance, but it was a good union shop, and Julian Warneke wouldn't have wanted anyone picketing his funeral.

7

"You going down to L.A. next week?"

"Yes." The "law school murders" trial was finally set to begin, and venue had been changed to Los Angeles. Unfortunately, I knew the murderer well; well enough to be the prosecution's main witness.

"This muddies the water." Surgelato squinted into the wind, watching a black limousine disgorge a youngish man in a dramatically shoulder-padded suit.

"What do you mean?"

"We never got a confession in that case. And you were a suspect. Now you're a suspect again."

"But this is completely unrelated—"

"Defense counsel will say *you're* the relationship. And much as I hate to say it, Di Palma's a hell of a lawyer."

Counsel for the defense was indeed a hell of a lawyer. And the fact that she'd pled her client not guilty didn't bode well.

"Maybe Julian wasn't—I mean, maybe the restaurant made an honest mistake."

"What do you know about hemlock, Miss Jansson?"

"Socrates drank some."

"That was from a tree—yew tree. This is a weed. Looks like a big carrot plant. A cubic inch of the root will kill you—after three or four hours. Mouth and tongue swell up. Malaise but no nausea." He inclined his head, watching me. "But you took botany at Stanford. I don't have to tell *you* this."

"All we did in Botany 1 was count sepals."

"Point is, you gotta go *find* hemlock. Disturbed ground near wetlands or woods. You don't just pick it up at the supermarket."

I could hear Brian Lieberman in the lobby of the chapel, discussing "power bicycling" with an attorney from the National Labor Relations Board. The shoulder-padded man from the limousine sauntered toward us. I turned my back on him.

"Heard you had a little trouble getting certified," the lieutenant observed.

"The bar association took its time investigating my background, if that's what you mean."

"Ah, yes, convicted of—"

"Resisting arrest." I smiled. "Those were the days."

"Warneke represented you, didn't he? Seems to me from looking at the arrest report, he could have plea bargained you down to—"

"Willa!" The shoulder-padded man laid a smooth white hand on my arm. "Long time! Great suit!" When I didn't reply, he persisted, "Don't you recognize me?"

If I hadn't, I wouldn't have turned my back on him.

Aaron Bancroft, who'd once led thousands of us in a march on Washington, now handed me his business card: *Consultant, The Elliot wave theory of stock market fluctuation.* I felt like throwing up.

Aaron's freckled, boy-next-door face had once seemed ironically incongruous with his radical views and wild hair. Now, with his trendy suit and big tortoiseshell glasses, Aaron looked like Howdy Doody grown up.

Luckily he spotted some other acquaintances and flitted off to give *them* his business card.

"*Networking* at a funeral!"

"You want my opinion?" I didn't, but Surgelato gave it to me anyway. "He's more useful to society this way than throwing Molotov cocktails at banks."

"Julian got him acquitted of that charge."

The lieutenant assumed an expression of mock ingenuousness. "Then he must have been innocent!"

Felix Flish ran up the mortuary steps, stopping short when he saw us. He extended his hand to Surgelato. "Sergeant!"

Surgelato's eyes were lost in the shadow of a jutting browbone, so I couldn't read his expression. "Glad you remember me from our talk the other night, Mr. Flish, but didn't I mention I'm a lieutenant?"

The wind whipped Felix's hair into something resembling a Kirlian aura. "Guess 'sergeant' is my default setting for policeman."

"Your—? Oh, I get it—a computer type." Judging from the lieutenant's tone, he didn't have much use for computer types.

Felix noticed me but failed to greet me, which was like him. He glanced into the chapel and smiled an oddly nostalgic smile. At the first notes of organ music, I followed him inside.

Julian's casket was surrounded by birds of paradise in stark Japanese arrangements. Before it, a group of women knelt sobbing. One of them was Bess Warneke, Julian's first wife. Another was Mae Siegel, the secretary Julian would have fired without compunction. The third was my mother.

Waddling down the aisle toward them was Silvio Bernstein, our congressman.

I couldn't believe my eyes.

I pushed through the crowd, intercepted Silvio, and pulled him into a dark corner behind the organ. A man in a clean, neatly pressed work shirt was playing "There'll Be Pie in the Sky When We Die (That's a Lie!)."

I had to put my lips to Silvio's fleshy ear to be heard—but not overheard. "What are *you* doing here?"

Silvio, a portly, perennially flushed man with only a few wisps of hair between him and baldness, intoned, "Julian Warneke was a deeply committed, highly responsible—"

"*Please!* You're supposed to be junketing—"

Silvio shook his head. "Didn't your father tell you? We postponed it until September."

"Jesus Christ!" I glanced anxiously at my mother. She and Bess were in a crying frenzy, knee deep in damp Kleenex. "Daddy packed up and went—*said* he was going with you. Mother thinks—"

Silvio's eyes widened. "I'll be!" Then he frowned. "This isn't like Willy at all!"

We looked at one another for a while, as if that would help us understand why my father had lied about going off to Nicaragua for two weeks.

• CHAPTER THREE •

My parents met at a Ban the Bomb meeting and conceived me shortly thereafter; this was probably the last thing they ever did that was unpreceded by moral debate. Getting married, they concluded, would be too bourgeois; and so my father was deprived of the hardship exemption that would have kept him out of the Korean War. Being much enamored of the passive-resistance philosophy of Mohandas Gandhi, he allowed himself to be trundled overseas, but refused to bear arms once he got there. He spent two years in a military stockade.

My mother, meanwhile, shocked her very respectable family by running off to Mexico to have her love child. She had a vague notion, I think, that this would make me bilingual.

By the time my father was dishonorably discharged, his parents, a Minnesota farm couple, had died and left him a brand-new blue-and-white Bel Air. I have a picture of myself sitting on the hood like a scraggly ornament. In the background are the badlands of Utah. My parents were On the Road.

When they, like others of the beat generation, got too old for the inconveniences of transiency, they settled in San Francisco, in what would later be called the Haight-Ashbury district. They enrolled me in a "school" that was actually the upstairs flat of a plump "candle artist" who smelled of incense and spoke in Zen koans (introducing me to the suspicion that Eastern philosophy makes people foolish).

My parents worked with retarded adults, which, I

suppose, helped them cope with the endless political meetings they attended.

By the time I was a teenager, our neighborhood had turned into a countercultural mecca. I liked a lot of things about it—notably the drugs and free love. When people began turning into "flower children" it got a little silly, but that's another story.

My mother's parents visited us once in 1968, in an attempt to reconcile with her. They concluded that my mother had married a shiftless nobody and raised a drug addict hippie prostitute. But unlike most of their generation, they opposed the Vietnam War, and all in all, we found them rather quaint. My parents, in what they termed an absurdist gesture, even went so far as to get married, just to please the grouchy pair. I missed most of the ceremony; I walked out when the barefoot, mail-order minister began reciting Kahlil Gibran's wedding doggerel. ("Now, Baby!" Mother chided me afterward, at the Tassajara Bakery. "He had his heart set on reading it!")

My grandparents returned the favor by leaving my mother a lot of money, most of which she donated to local soup kitchens. My parents were soon broke again, but as my father observed, they could always count on a hot meal at Saint Anthony's.

When the liberalism petered out, leaving us with Jimmy Carter, my parents (virtually his only supporters) took up human rights as their cause. This led to a stint in the Peace Corps and also started them gallivanting around Central America in time for a series of bloody insurrections. I may as well have had mercenaries for parents; every time I read about a bloodbath south of the border, I knew my parents were there.

The only other Americans in such places at such times were Catholic missionaries, and my mother was soon converted. This meant, among other things, a second, Catholic wedding (no Kahlil Gibran, at least), and a sudden proliferation of icons among the NO MORE VIETNAMS posters in their living room. My mother also confided to me that she'd stopped using birth control, but as she was in the middle of menopause, the action was largely symbolic. ("And I still pro-choice, of *course*!")

My father, a short slender man with a receding hairline, great cheekbones, and dimples (which I inherited), is still handsome, for a man his age. But in my own prejudiced opinion, he is too committed to my mother and their bleeding-heart causes to have the time or the inclination to begin philandering so late in life.

So when he told us his boyhood chum, now Congressman Silvio Bernstein, was taking him along on a fact-finding junket to Nicaragua, we believed him. My mother said, rather wistfully, that she supposed she could stand her own cooking for two weeks. But aside from a few tears and a severe warning not to let Silvio co-opt him (she had yet to forgive the congressman for supporting the death penalty bill), Mother displayed little anxiety when my father departed.

And though he'd made his usual fuss about not letting us accompany him to the airport, he certainly hadn't acted nervous or guilty.

So where the hell was he?

• CHAPTER FOUR •

After the funeral we caravanned to Brian Lieberman's vineyard, BMWs following ancient psychedelic vans and Teamster tractors. I rode with Felix Flish in his black Saab. He made no effort to converse with me. Instead, he put on a Rolling Stones tape and kept time by cracking his big toe. It took me fifteen minutes to figure out the sound came from his French-bread-sized shoe, and another fifteen to talk myself out of stomping on his foot.

When the tape ended, I jumped into the breach, hoping to stave off side two. "Why do you guys want to fire Mae?"

"Don't put that turd in *my* pocket—*I* don't want to fire her!"

"Well, why does Clement—?"

"Mae's sleeping with Jim Zissner."

Jim Zissner was running for Teamsters Local 16's highest office, secretary-treasurer. Local 16, Clement's biggest client, was known for the acrimony of its elections. This year's was particularly savage, with Zissner's Teamsters for a Democratic Union accusing the current secretary-treasurer, Semi Sawyer, of everything but vampirism. Clement had little regard for the TDU; I'd once heard him sneer, "If they want democracy, they should try negotiating individual contracts!"

"And you know what a fucking paranoid Sawyer is," Felix continued. "He's saying Zissner has a spy in our office."

Though our office ostensibly represented all members of Local 16, the local's will was finally and immutably expressed

15

by its secretary-treasurer. Semi Sawyer alone decided which grievances our firm filed and which we ignored. Many of his other executive decisions—to strike, to tacitly approve anti-scab "incidents," and to honor other unions' picket lines, for example—also generated legal complications. That's why Sawyer authorized payment of a yearly retainer fee to our firm. In return, he expected his consultations with us to remain confidential, even—perhaps especially—from his fellow Teamsters.

"Mae wouldn't pass on confidential information!"

"Try telling Semi—it's like talking to Krakatoa. And Clement's throwing around phrases like 'appearance of impropriety' and 'conflict of interest.'"

"Clement should be *defending* Mae!"

Felix grinned wryly.

"Felix, it's feudal! Clement has no right to tell the secretaries who they can and can't sleep with! If Semi can't prove—"

"You gonna explain the rules of evidence to Semi? Or tell Mr. Labor Law who he's entitled to fire?"

Felix flipped over the Stones tape and snapped it back into the tape deck, ensuring his question would remain rhetorical. Between the music and the toe cracking, I felt like I was rolling to Brian's vineyard in a barrel.

The vineyard was a cultivated little hillside with a boxy structure at the foot and a huge Victorian farmhouse at the top. The house, which Brian called Timely Manor, had a covered veranda along three sides. On it were several mauve-clothed tables. From them, young men in matadorlike catering uniforms took up trays of stuffed mushrooms and crudités and scattered.

Uphill from me, potbellied Teamsters emitted clouds of cigar smoke and passed around a liter bottle of Jack Daniels, which they poured into emptied wine glasses. As I came closer, I could hear them discussing the indictment of

Teamsters International's latest president. The words "set up" and "union busting" were repeated several times, angrily. Then, abruptly, their conversation stopped. Teamster dissident Jim Zissner had joined them.

Into this tinderbox waltzed a young matador, murmuring, "French plums dipped in white chocolate?"

Semi Sawyer, looking uncomfortably large in his cheap suit, stepped back as if he'd been offered used condoms.

Zissner, a lanky man with Semitic features, smiled wolfishly. "'Fraid to try something new, Semi?"

"If it looks like sugarcoated dog shit, I am!" Semi's supporters hooted with laughter.

"Calling it dog shit doesn't make it less delicious." Zissner took one off the tray and popped it into his mouth.

"Whatever it is, it ain't my style!" Sawyer turned around and noticed me behind him. I'd represented Local 16 on a number of minor matters, but he didn't acknowledge my presence. The fact that a cute little blonde could get his local off the hook and save it money didn't make her a real lawyer; Sawyer considered himself liberal for not holding Clement Kerrey's beard against him. I suppose I should have minded, but I didn't.

I walked uphill toward the house and noticed Felix Flish talking to Aaron Bancroft. I was about to join them when a matador blocked my path, thrusting a trayful of wineglasses in my face. I took a glass, slipped past him, and almost collided with Aaron, who'd stepped hastily away from Felix. Bancroft blinked at me, looking equal parts perplexed and irritated. Without speaking, he continued downhill, toward the parked cars.

"What was that about?"

Felix watched Aaron flee, the corners of his mouth curling with dreamy satisfaction. "Nothing, really." He took my arm and we moved toward the house. "Wonder how our precious Brian affords this place."

The house gleamed with waxed hardwoods and filtered light from latticed windows. Mustachioed men stood behind polished oak bars pouring Harpsichord (Brian's label) wine. Flowery signs urged us to visit the wine cellar and pointed us toward the stairs. Felix was about to precede me down them when Matthilde Warneke, Julian's latest wife, came dashing up them. She saw Felix but she didn't see me, trailing behind him. She gasped, "Oh, Feeelix!" and hurled herself into his arms.

Felix said something like, "My condolences," but the real message was in his brief but sensuous embrace.

Matthilde stepped back, saw me, and quickly looked down, her thick lashes like visors over her eyes. She slowly shrugged the folds of her black-caped dress back into place. Matthilde and I had gone to law school together. We hadn't liked each other then and we didn't like each other now.

She was a tall, shapely woman with waist-length black hair, hollow cheeks, huge brown eyes and a breathy voice I'd heard described as sexy. She began fingering a tiny upside-down gold cross pinned over her heart. In our second year of law school, Matthilde had embraced witchcraft because it represented an ancient tradition of worshiping female deities. (I'd just as soon blame things on a male one, myself.)

"How are you, Willa?" The cross apparently provided the necessary comfort; her tone was calm. "And how is—what was his name? From school?"

"That's history." It had taken a twenty-six-day explosion to kill it, but it was dead.

Matthilde shrugged. "Oh. He didn't really seem like your type."

I excused myself and went down the stairs. I don't much like discussing my romantic failures.

Brian Lieberman stood at the foot of the stairs greeting new arrivals. He looked as manicured and content as ever in his tuxedo. He touched his cheek to mine and, with a wave of the arm, indicated the people assembled in his cathedrallike cellar. "It's quite a tribute to Julian, isn't it? Working men and women, politicians, pacifists, lawyers from all over the state." He spoke with the satisfaction of a man saying, "Great party!" Then he turned his back on me to greet a new arrival; he was working the funeral.

I looked around the vast, spotless cavern, with its daylight windows and walls of stacked bottles. I noticed my mother standing in the middle of the room beside Bess Warneke.

I joined them, kissing Mother's teary cheek and extending my hand to Bess. She was a plump woman with extraordinarily beautiful blue eyes. Her makeup was understated, her gray hair was "done" into a sleek helmet, and her blue knit suit was complemented by matching burgundy pumps, handbag, and scarf. (Looking at her, Felix had once corrupted the old union slogan, "Don't mourn; organize," into "Don't mourn; accessorize.") As far as anyone knew, the only thing wrong with Bess's marriage to Julian had been that Bess was—and looked—sixty.

I was expressing my condolences when I noticed Mother gaping at something on the stair. I glanced over my shoulder, then reeled forward, stomping my mother's sore toes and forcing a pained squeal out of her.

And that made *him* look over at us.

For a moment Edward Hershey looked as surprised as I was; then a half smile spread over his face. I'd have liked to wipe it off with the heel of my shoe.

He tucked his hands into his jacket pockets and stood there jingling his change, looking at me. My mother was saying something, but I didn't quite catch it. I was looking at the last man on earth I wanted to see.

Hershey was tall, maybe six-one, big through the chest, small in the hips, very long legged. He wore a corduroy sport jacket over an Izod shirt, blue jeans, not too faded, and Frye boots. The uniform looked casual, but it had certainly set him back a few bucks. And so had the messed-curl haircut.

He looked older: fifteen years is a long time. But he'd always had a rough face, jaw too square, eyes squinty, nose crooked, five o'clock shadow. But the bastard didn't need good looks, he had pheromones.

Two women I didn't know, one a snooty-looking redhead and the other an all-business brunette, fluttered toward him.

And my mother, in a voice that could have shattered glass, finally succeeded in getting my attention. "Baby! It's that boy from Boston who gave you the—"

"Mother!"

She clapped her hands to her face, gasping, "Oh, goodness!" Then, noticing Bess Warneke's shocked expression, she giggled.

I'm sure it was clear to Bess what Edward Hershey had given me.

A moment later, I felt his hand on my shoulder.

"You're all grown up!" he drawled.

I jerked free. "What are *you* doing here?"

"Julian kept me out of jail, remember?" He extended a hand to Bess. "Mrs. Warneke, what can I say? He kept me out of hell; that's how I feel about him."

A stirring tribute, considering Julian had counseled the usual theatrical jury trial and Hershey had instead insisted on plea bargaining.

I didn't hear what Bess said; I was looking at Edward goddam Hershey and not so discreetly pushing Mother away from us. She made a few disgruntled noises, but finally took the hint, joining a nearby folksinger and her defrocked priest husband. I heard them thank her for the banana bread.

Edward was saying, "Santa Cruz. Been there for two years now. Here's my card, just in case." He handed Bess a business card; apparently networking at funerals was the done thing.

Bess glanced at the card and then at him—inimically, until

he smiled, the bastard. She murmured, "I don't think so—I don't see the need," then she turned away, leaving us alone.

It was like getting sucked into a time warp, something my landlord assures me is quite common. 1972; Willa in love; that one had ended in explosion, too.

"Come on, Willa! Can't we let bygones—?" Hershey caught my shoulder before I could depart. "Haven't you ever been tempted to skip the spiel? When you were sure—"

"*Sure* my ass!"

I noticed Clement Kerrey standing behind Edward, frowning at me, lips pinched till they'd disappeared behind his mustache. He turned back to the state senator with whom he'd been chatting. He'd be firing *me* next, I supposed.

I knocked Edward's hand off my shoulder and left the cellar, bumping into Bess at the top of the stair.

She was studying Edward's card.

• CHAPTER FIVE •

When I got back from Los Angeles eight days later, my mother was in a twitter.

"Oh, Baby! You'll never guess!"

I pushed past her into the flat, which smelled of take-out pizza. "That's a safe bet."

"It's his will!"

I glanced at a large icon, sandwiched between posters shouting NO MORE VIETNAMS and NICARAGUA FOR THE NICARAGUANS. It showed a stylized and very swarthy Jesus.

"No, no! *Julian's* will."

"That what?"

"That left me the house!"

"Oh, his *will*! What house? Why would Julian leave you guys—?"

"Just me." My mother blushed and turned away. "I can't imagine!"

Had it not been for the blush, I couldn't have imagined either. I looked at my saggy, unkempt mother and wondered if anyone other than Daddy could possibly find her sexy.

"Julian left you a house? Where?"

She kept her back to me, stooping to gather up a stack of paperbacks. "*His* house."

"As in, the house his wife lives in? The one his kids expect to sell and divide the proceeds of? *That* house?"

Mother dumped her armload of books into a box at the

foot of the bookcase (Daddy insists on shelving them himself, as Mother organizes them by height of spine).

"You never liked Julian!" Her tone had a disturbing why-can't-you-get-along-with-your-stepfather quality. "You never let him be a real *friend* to you."

"That's not fair!" I wasn't a tears-in-public kind of person, but I'd known Julian as long as I could remember. His letter of recommendation had helped me get into law school. And contrary to what Lieutenant Surgelato had implied, I hadn't held it against Julian when his theatrics goaded Judge Rondi into giving me two months for making an obscene suggestion (figurative, of course) to a military cop. "Julian was—*older*. Not to mention my boss."

A few noble tears (Mother's specialty) trickled down her cheeks.

"Besides, you're avoiding the issue. Why would Julian leave *you* his house?"

"I've known him a long time," she replied noncommittally.

"So have his children. Were you lovers?"

I was relieved to see her look aghast. "Baby!"

"What then? Did he owe you money?"

"You're always so suspicious! Remember how you accused those nice Osbournes of being after our money? And at *dinner*, too!"

"Well, have you heard another word about the Fund for Starving Debutantes, or whatever the hell—"

"Now, you *see*! That's exactly what I mean! It was an *educational* program, for children of the upper—"

"You're changing the subject!"

"—to help them develop a social conscience." Her cheeks glowed with indignation.

"Julian has three sons. And a bunch of bratty grandchildren he complains about. Complained about. An ex-wife he lived with for twenty-some years and another wife still under warranty. Why the hell should he leave his house to a casual friend?"

"Maybe he wanted to be sure it would be used for the good of—"

"The masses. I don't know how to break this to you, Mother, but Julian was as *effete* as—"

"I can't think how you turned out so—"

"—any Republican!"

My mother gasped. "Now that really is enough, Willa!" She stalked out of the room, pausing at the door to glance at me reprovingly.

• CHAPTER SIX •

I sat on the floor manicuring some pot and watching Ronald Reagan on my landlord's television. Ronnie had just outlined a quintessentially Republican plan to spend billions arresting drug addicts while simultaneously defunding their treatment centers. His dried herring of a wife (this was a "joint" message) smiled her wan smile and applauded a teenager who'd sicced the cops on her drug-using parents. A few months earlier she'd displayed public fury with her own daughter for invading *her* privacy by writing a novel about the First Family.

"By the Mighty Moons, I'm glad I never whelped!" My landlord, a beer-bellied, sixtyish hippie who viewed life as a science-fiction epic, handed me the Zig-Zags.

"It's all I can do to keep my parents *out* of jail!"

"But you see," he lowered his voice solemnly, "they're all around us!" What I saw all around us were posters of Arnold Schwarzenegger types hacking tentacles off aliens with dripping teeth. "It won't be long now!"

I tossed him the joint. Ben Bubniak was one of the hundred and forty-four thousand who would be spared the horrors of the Apocalypse (or so his friend Hasim the Wizard assured him, whenever he came to fix the plumbing); I, on the other hand, could not face The End without a few hits of pot. I struck a match.

Ben, breath held, smoke sliding over the lank, slush-gray hair that hung to his shoulders, reached for the TV's remote control. Ron and Nancy were exchanging smarmy smiles and a voice-over was saying, "Stay tuned for Channel Four News; tonight's *Segment Four:* 'A Requiem for a Radical, Part Five'; a sixties reunion at the wake of Julian Warneke." Ben pressed the mute button.

"Did you go to the wake, Earth Woman?"

"Yes."

He handed me the joint. "Perhaps we'll see you on the news."

"God, I hope not! I was on the news after I testified in L.A. I looked like I'd spent the night under a bridge. My hair—"

"What's that lawyer like?"

"Di Palma almost convinced me *I'd* done it. It gave me the creeps." I felt my fingers begin to knot themselves into my hair, remembered how I'd looked on TV, and forced myself to stop. "I wonder if I'll ever be that good."

"Let's hope not."

"My parents didn't want me to become a lawyer. They didn't want me to become part of a system that punishes lofty gestures like putting dents in missile nose cones." I took a hit, spoke with breath held. "I suppose that's why I did it."

"Because it's immoral?" His tone told me that was all right, too; with the Apocalypse at hand, he could afford to be generous. As long as I didn't Bogart the joint.

"They used to make me feel so *exposed*. Mother'd see a cop car pull up outside and she'd hustle me out the back door—when I was little I used to think the cops were after *me*. I'd go cower at Lissa's until they phoned for me to come home. Then I'd find Mother and Daddy agonizing about whether posting bail had compromised their morals."

"But you like the law biz, don't you?" He sleepily watched the muted television.

I shrugged, taking back the joint. "A few months ago, I nagged Clement Kerrey into giving me some of his cases.

Union labor law; absolutely politically correct, right? You know what I'm working on now? This Filipino widow, her husband was a Teamster for twenty years with one four-month layoff. The union says the layoff kept his pension from vesting."

Ben whistled, shaking his head. The Second Coming was at hand; how would I explain screwing a widow out of her husband's pension?

"And you know what?" The smoke seared my lungs, but it was worth it; things were looking better. The Filipino widow was just another martyr to the great god of Irony. "Now Mother's into women becoming 'empowered.' She shows all her friends my résumé."

Ben's watery eyes were fixed lasciviously on Channel Four's anchorwoman. I extended the joint, but he didn't take it. I kept on smoking. I'd been doing a lot of smoking since I'd started working for Julian.

Still smoking, I trudged upstairs to my own flat.

There were stockings and newspapers on my futon couch; my floor was littered with crumpled letters, shoes, books, legal pads, and empty microwave pouches with plastic forks still stuck inside. But the place had looked a lot worse. On the third day of the bar exam Ripley himself wouldn't have believed it.

I finished the joint.

I'd spent the previous week in a Los Angeles courtroom reliving—and all but being accused of—the murder of three law school friends. Never mind that the real murderer had almost killed *me*, too; in her closing statement, defense counsel argued that silly little me had misinterpreted the accused's intentions.

In addition, my boss, my old friend, was dead, and, judging from the mail I'd been getting, people thought I'd killed him (the mail was bound to increase when people learned the terms of his will); my parents were lying to me, and, it appeared, to each other; the love of my life had threatened to punch me in the nose if he ever saw me again; and Edward goddam Hershey was back in town.

Sitting in the quiet chaos of my apartment, I dared to think things couldn't get any worse. Then Don Surgelato showed up.

"Got a minute, Miss Jansson?"

"You've come for a urine specimen."

"A *what*?"

"Didn't you see *der Fuehrer*'s speech?"

"I've been working."

"You look it."

"I got a call from L.A." Surgelato stepped into the room, patting his pockets. His usually olive complexion was cancer-ward beige. "Jury just returned a verdict: voluntary manslaughter." He flopped down on the futon, absently pushing away some hoisery. "Heat of passion, my badge! Murderer prowls around your law school—how many months?—killing people off, and some shyster—excuse me, *lawyer*—convinces the jury there was no premeditation. Jesus Christ!"

I stood there for a while, less surprised by the verdict than by the lieutenant's unprofessional demeanor. Did he think the trial made us pals?

"That's not why I came here, though." Surgelato patted his pockets again; a fellow ex-smoker, I recognized the search for phantom cigarettes. "We need you at the Hall. Thought you might like a lift."

"Can it wait until morning?"

"Nothing waits until morning. I thought we'd swing by and pick up your mother. June Jansson, that's your mother, isn't it?"

I was tempted to deny it, and not for the first time. The lieutenant stood up, jerking his neck as if to relieve tight muscles. "Eccentric lady, from what they tell me. Fifteen arrests—pouring blood on draft files, blocking the entrance to—"

"Not eccentric—committed."

He shrugged. "I can respect that. Sure." But as I pulled my coat off a chair he added, "Wish people would respect the effing *law* as much as we respect their effing rights!"

• CHAPTER SEVEN •

Mother was doing her passive-resistance number on Surgelato. She lay limply on the floor at his feet. The lieutenant looked at me, and sighed.

It was a wasted sigh. "You can't really make her talk to you if she doesn't want to."

"We're talking to all Warneke's heirs. Tell her we're not singling her out!"

"Lieutenant, she's protesting, she's not deaf."

He looked down at her inert form. "Mrs. Jansson—"

"*Ms.* Jansson."

Surgelato sighed again. "Ms. Jansson, it's my job to find out who poisoned Julian Warneke. If I don't talk to the people who knew him . . ." He spread his arms helplessly.

Mother sat up. "What about the Blue Fox?" The Blue Fox was a lesbian bar the police had raided the previous evening.

Surgelato looked perplexed. "The Fox? What about it? Owners were selling cocaine, as I understand it. What's the Fox got to do with—"

"Everything!" my mother proclaimed, legs straight in front of her and hands on her hips as if she were about to practice yoga. "It has *everything* to do with it! Here you are pretending you care about Julian, and what are you doing but trampling all over the things he stood for!" She glared at him through outraged tears, then lay back down.

I settled into a chair to wait. All we needed were a few choruses of "We Shall Overcome."

"Look, Mrs.—*Ms.*—Jansson, Julian Warneke left you property valued at three-quarters of a million dollars, and we're naturally curious—"

Mother gasped and sat up again. "Three-quarters of a million!" She frowned. "That's *terrible!*"

Seeing Surgelato's expression, I explained, "Amassing capital instead of spending it on worthy causes."

"Is that what you intend to do with the property, Ms. Jansson? Spend it on—"

"He couldn't have known it was worth so much!"

"I told you Julian was a capitalist, Mother!"

"Hush!" Mother crossed herself. "I won't have you speaking ill of the dead! It's just a *small* house—"

"A block from the marina," the lieutenant pointed out. "You can't buy a garage in that neighborhood for less than two hundred thousand. Now please, Ms. Jansson, we'd appreciate your cooperation." Mother reclined, snorting. "You know, if I wanted to, I could send a marked unit out here and have you pulled in as a suspect." He waited for her to respond.

Mother closed her eyes, shaking her limbs slightly to relax them.

"Don't send anyone with a hernia or back trouble," I advised.

He glanced at me, then looked back down at my mother, studying her ancient sweater and jeans, her sags and wrinkles and unbrushed hair. He shook his head slightly. "*You'll* come along, I hope, Miss Jansson."

"No, she won't!" Mother snapped, opening her eyes.

I preceded the lieutenant out to his unmarked Ford Fairlane.

"Interesting lady," he commented tactfully. "Must have known Julian Warneke a long time."

I stood with my hand on the car door, looking down a

street of shared-wall Victorian apartment buildings, most of them needing paint. At the corner, a spike-haired punk took something from a pony-tailed old man in Birkenstocks. Across the street, a neighbor parked in the tiny garage for which he paid an extra hundred dollars a month.

My mother had known Julian Warneke for twenty-five years, give or take; but so had a lot of other people.

"Give me a minute alone with her, Lieutenant."

Surgelato was silent, the streetlamp above him casting his eyes into a visor of shadow. Taking advantage of his hesitation, I dashed back up the steps, letting myself in with my key.

Mother was on the hallway phone, her back to me. In much the same tone as Matthilde Warneke, she bleated, "Oh, Feeelix!" Then she glanced over her shoulder and noticed me.

She replaced the receiver in its cradle. She blinked at me, pushing hair off her forehead. "I thought you were going with that awful—! I'm glad you didn't—!"

"He's waiting outside."

She hugged herself, her stretched-out turtleneck apparently failing to keep her warm. Her hair was light gray streaked with yellow blond; her skin was lined from sunburnt forays to Liberia, Colombia, El Salvador, Cuba, and the Philippines. Her blue eyes were pretty, but not excessively so; her nose was on the large side; her uncolored lips wrinkled when she talked. Braless (as she was now) she looked too skinny on top and too broad beneath. This was not a woman for whose sake a man disinherits two wives and three children.

"What have you done, Mother? Tell me so I can back you up."

For a millisecond her eyes flashed with pride in me; I'd seen the look thousands of times. What worried me was the expression that replaced it.

"For god's sake, Mother! If you can't trust *me*, who can you trust?" I glanced at the phone. "*Not* Felix Flish!"

Mother turned her back on me.

"Why did you call Felix? What does he have to do with this? Did you two forge Julian's will?"

"No!" She reached behind the telephone table to retrieve a pencil, dusting off her fingers as she straightened up.

"Did you—or Felix—blackmail Julian into—?"

The buzzer sounded and Mother dropped the pencil again.

I opened the door, expecting to see the bullish Surgelato. Instead, bent beneath his duffel bag, stood my grinning father.

"Where on earth have you *been*, Daddy?"

And he said, "Why, Nicaragua, of course!"

• CHAPTER EIGHT •

Felix Flish reclined in his vinyl executive chair, his back to me, his fingers laced behind his head. A few inches of furry wrist stuck out of each sleeve; his collar was hiked into hair so coarse it resembled a scrub brush. His shoeless feet were crossed atop a scatter of file folders on the desk, and his socks were a trifle too woolly for his suit. On one side of him, a narrow window framed a portion of the parking garage across the street; he seemed to find the view absorbing. Words in business-letter format lit his computer terminal. Squinting, I could make out the phrase "declaratory relief."

He said, "I believe it's customary to clear your throat."

"Um-hum-hum."

He dropped his feet to the floor, swiveling to face me. "Have I ever seen you in the office this early before?"

"No, and you never will again." I felt like death on toast. "I want to talk to you."

"One minute." He hunched over his computer keyboard, tapping out a few commands. The screen went blank. "I'm all yours."

I sat in a low-backed version of Felix's chair. I could hear traffic sounds from the street below; it was six-thirty in the morning—rush hour had begun. "I was at the Hall of Justice till eleven o'clock last night." The revelation that I might benefit, through Mother, from Julian's death, had fascinated two teams of homicide inspectors.

"Yeah?" Felix looked interested. "With The Surge?"

There didn't seem to be a man alive who didn't recall Surgelato's "broken-field running," whatever that might be. "Yes. But that's not what I want to talk to you about. My mother phoned you last night."

He raised his brows. Because his nose had no indentation at the bridge, it made him look a little like a collie. "Do I know your mother?"

"I had a feeling you'd lie about it."

"Am I supposed to have something going with her? Your father's not on his way here with a shotgun, is he?" Felix seemed relaxed, amused. It struck a sour note—maybe because he was talking about my mother.

"Have you seen Julian's will?"

"Yup. He left his cash to his wife and his house to some lady named— Aha! Your mother!" He rolled his chair closer to me.

"Even if you don't know her yourself, which you must, Clement would have told you who she was. Clement's known her for years."

"Clement's been a little peeved with me lately, you may have noticed. We don't spend a great deal of time chatting."

Felix had been with the law firm only two years, but Julian had recently insisted he be made partner. Rumor (via my secretary, Mae) had it that Clement and Brian had voted "no" to early partnership for Felix, but that Julian had somehow pulled rank and demanded his way. Losing what Mae called "yet another" power struggle with Julian had infuriated Clement; the mere mention of Felix as partner still sent Clement stiffly out of the room.

"Basically"—Felix picked up a mechanical pencil and bounced it off its eraser—"Julian was an old goat. Here, I'll show you." He tapped at his computer keyboard again, responding to a few terse questions on the screen. A document lit the terminal. "Page one of Julian's will. Juli had Mae type it into the system for him."

I peered at the green letters. A collection of wines and brandies to Brian Lieberman, a racehorse (I was surprised to learn) to Clement Kerrey. Felix pushed a button to replace page one with page two. A couple of bank accounts for Matthilde, some corny sentiments for his children, and sure enough, his house to my mother. "I suppose Mae remembers typing this? I mean, if there'd been any changes, she'd have noticed."

Felix's smile was full of delighted mischief. "Ever watched Mae type? She goes too fast to read what she's working on."

I could hear the reception room phones ringing. I checked my wristwatch: six-fifty. The reporters were up early.

"But—" Felix pressed the blinking button on his phone. "Julian presumably read what he was signing, so—" He picked up the receiver. "Warneke, Kerrey, Lieberman & Flish."

For a moment Felix was silent, staring at his terminal.

I stifled a yawn. I was trying to cut down on coffee; it had a way of turning me into a banshee by afternoon. But, Jesus, at this hour I could hardly sit up straight without it.

Then Felix said, "Appreciate it," and hung up.

He leaned back in his chair, closing his eyes and taking a deep breath.

"What's the matter?"

"Zissner. Jim Zissner." He opened his eyes to a wince. "You know him, don't you? Teamsters for a Democratic Union guy? Running against Sawyer in the Local 16—?"

"Of course I know Zissner. What did he do?"

"He went over Devil's Slide in his Trans-Am last night." Felix loosened his tie, his long face suddenly rather clammy. "He's dead. They think a truck tractor might have forced him off the road."

"A truck!" I sat there numbly for a while, listening to the phones ring. "So a Teamster—a Local 16 man—might have— Oh, shit!"

"In quantity, and on our side of the fan."

• CHAPTER NINE •

Clement Kerrey stabbed his fork into an uneaten oriental chicken salad. He wore a navy blue suit with brass buttons, a light blue shirt, a deep red tie. His dark gray hair and beard were neatly clipped; his black eyes glittered under straight, gray-white brows. Beside him, Brian Lieberman leaned back in the leather-upholstered booth, one arm draped over its back. But Clement sat like a Victorian lady, as he would have in the more elegant restaurant Julian had generally chosen.

Felix said what was on all our minds. "It's no use keeping the shop open. We've got reporters every place but the toilet bowl. Let's re-drape the door till Monday."

After Julian's death, Mae Siegel had hung black crepe over the door. On a black-bordered card she'd typed, *In respect for the memory of*, et cetera, *we will be closed*, et cetera. Today, we'd have to do our own typing. Mae had been shocked into catatonia when we'd told her about Zissner; the gossip about them had been true. I'd taken her home in a taxi and then summoned her best friend, a grade-school teacher, to Mae's Sunset District apartment.

Mae had waited tearlessly for the teacher, her round, half-Chinese face showing more anger than sorrow at the death of her lover. I intruded on her grief long enough to ask a few questions about Julian's will.

When her friend arrived, Mae informed her, with simple fury, "They killed him! The bastards murdered Jim!" Then she'd looked at me and croaked, "Go away!"

Now, Clement pounded the table once, with a fury rivaling Mae's. "He's lying!"

There was little doubt to whom Clement referred. A resident of Montara claimed to have seen a truck tractor—the kind that hooks up to a semi—follow Zissner's Trans-Am onto the serpentine cliff road known as Devil's Slide. The Montara man had particularly noticed it, he told the police, because trucks rarely attempt that road.

I'd seen Clement Kerrey furious only once before, when Ronald Reagan had busted the air traffic controllers' union. Kerrey's outrage—or more accurately, the fact that a lawyer could be so passionate about his practice—had been one of the reasons I'd applied to law school.

Brian Lieberman, freshly tanned (he'd obviously spent his week of mourning in the sunshine of his vineyard), looked around the restaurant with evident embarrassment. "We'll find out if he is. Don't worry."

Felix shook his head. "Face it, Clement, the Teamsters have a thuggy image, and people are going to believe the worst no matter what you say. Cops'll never prove Local 16 had anything to do with it, but you'll never disprove it, either. Point is, it doesn't matter one way or the other. As long as the local can hold onto its members and negotiate decent contracts for them—"

The waiter rolled the dessert cart over to our table, and while a busboy cleared away our dishes, he recited the full catalog of artery cloggers. The last time we'd listened to someone do that, Julian had been with us. When the waiter pointed with pride to a parfait glass of amaretto mousse, Clement slid out of the booth and left the restaurant.

"And not a tear to spare for Zissner, the poor bastard," I heard Felix murmur.

Brian wadded up his serviette and tossed it onto the table. "Oh, Christ! Spare us the sanctimony!" He followed Clement out.

Our waiter looked startled. Felix grinned at him. "Guess they didn't want to pick up the tab."

"Don't you wish us to bill your—?"

"Bad joke." Felix extended a long, bony hand for the bill, computed a fifteen percent tip, to the penny, and signed for the lunch. "You going back to the office, Willa?"

"I have to. I'm screwing a widow out of her Teamsters' pension this afternoon."

"Ain't it grand, having a social conscience?"

Out on the street, I caught Felix's arm. An army of wool-suited workers flowed around us. "If you can call up Julian's will on your computer, then you know how to make changes in it." Car horns popped like firecrackers in the lunch hour traffic. "And I don't believe you about my mother."

Felix did not appear offended; he merely raised his brows, his long face again resembling Lassie's. "Am I missing something? You don't want your mother to inherit Juli's house?"

"Did you alter the will, Felix?"

"I told you, Mae typed it. I doubt if anyone but her knew the terms—if she knew them."

"She told me she didn't. Julian had her type a template. He filled in the names himself. She showed him how to do that on the computer. And how to print out a copy."

"Well, there you go. I doubt if anyone but Mae even knew it was on line—Julian wouldn't have told anybody."

"There were two witnesses, weren't there? That's what the probate code requires. They might have known."

"Mae witnessed Julian's signature." He smiled.

"Who else?"

"Me." His eyes sparkled as he watched me consider the implications of this. "But the fact remains, I do *not* know your mother!"

• CHAPTER TEN •

It was six o'clock. I'd been bending my elbow at a tawdry Mexican bar with a Teamsters business agent. He'd shown up at City Hall, second-floor Superior Court, to hear me persuade the judge to dismiss the Filipino widow's lawsuit. I'd expected Semi Sawyer, but the business agent confided that Sawyer was miffed with Clement for turning the case over to me.

The business agent was better company anyway. Though he agreed the widow'd gotten what he called "the Phillips screw," he was fanatically committed to saving the union money (the locals were all painstakingly thrifty; it was the International that believed in interest-free "loans" to its officers and their friends). As far as the business agent was concerned, I'd earned part of the small (to them it seemed large) annual retainer they paid our firm. He didn't mention the death of Jim Zissner, except to wave his leg-of-mutton arm and slur, "Devils for a Democratic Hell, har har."

I had the business agent drop me off at my office (to my question, "Are you sure you can drive?" he'd suavely replied, "Does a pig roll in shit?"). The office building was unlocked; it would be until eight. Our suite of offices on the third floor was locked up, as it always was after six.

I unlocked the door and walked through the reception area, a windowless quadrangle of dusty carpet, vinyl couches, and abstract acrylics. Phones were ringing, but no one was around to answer them; the way I felt, that included me. I

41

passed Julian's office and almost fainted when I saw his door ajar. I heard the toilet of his tiny private bathroom flush.

A moment later, Bess Warneke stepped out of the bathroom and into Julian's office. Julian's first wife was wearing an impeccably accessorized blue knit suit. She was crying, heaving with silent tears. Her nose was red and her lipstick was smeared. Her gray helmet of hair was mashed beneath a blue silk scarf. She sat at Julian's desk and dropped a key into the drawer. Then she hugged her handbag, slumping over it. She looked old.

She didn't see me, and I didn't see much point in announcing myself. Bess was the kind of lady who'd feel obliged to begin redoing her makeup and hair, and I wasn't audience enough for that kind of effort.

I tiptoed to my office, quietly shutting the door behind me. My desk was littered with telephone messages in Brian and Clement's secretary's handwriting. Maria was a dignified sausage of a woman with a slight Italian accent; her writing was cramped and curlicued, very European.

Surgelato had called; so had my mother. So had both San Francisco papers and a reporter friend of mine. So had Channels Two, Four, Five, and Seven. And so had Matthilde Warneke.

Here's why I hate Matthilde Jarvis Warneke: At eight forty-five A.M., every school day of my first year of law school, a hundred and thirty of us seated ourselves alphabetically in an amphitheater-shaped classroom. Matthilde Jarvis sat directly to my right, in the seventh row. Below us sat a forty-year-old former documentary filmmaker named Bill Ingram.

Ingram was a lanky man with muscular arms, a snide voice, and drop-dead eyes. He was renowned among lefties for a film called *The Night of March Nineteenth*. The film profiled Martin Rittenhaus, a radical lawyer who'd vanished in 1971 after allegedly smuggling a gun to his incarcerated Black

Panther client, Harlen Pryce. The film preached to the converted that Rittenhaus hadn't been fool enough to do any such thing; that prison authorities had framed him so as to defuse the prison-reform movement he'd led.

At the time of his disappearance, Rittenhaus had been Julian Warneke's law partner. He'd represented my mother once, and Mother, who rents movies from the public library and inflicts them on her guests in lieu of dessert, had shown the film at least ten times.

The fifth or sixth time Mother showed the movie, I began to wonder if she had a crush on Rittenhaus; but then, most lefties did. Rittenhaus hadn't been particularly handsome (it was hard to tell, under the beard and big glasses), but he'd kept a lot of radicals out of jail, and his sardonic, quotable sense of humor had allowed Bill Ingram to turn him into a cult hero.

Matthilde Jarvis had known I was sleeping with Bill Ingram. I didn't know she knew it, not until I found out she was sleeping with him, too. I immediately broke off the sexual part of my relationship with Bill (I'd have preferred to break off part of his anatomy). Appearances required me to display greater sophistication and sangfroid than I possessed, however; and I was required to do it for most of a school year. During that time, Matthilde told me at regular intervals that either she or Bill had slept with someone else, but that it hadn't affected *their* relationship. I guess I didn't actually *hate* Matthilde, though, until she alluded sympathetically to the problem I'd acquired from Edward Hershey.

I could hear Bess Warneke prowling Julian's office, and I wondered if Matthilde had been equally kind to *her* when she'd stolen Julian.

I crumpled the pink slip of paper with Matthilde's phone number and dropped it into my wastepaper basket. However and whyever Mother had accomplished it, Julian's will would at least evict Matthilde.

I picked up the phone to answer my reporter friend's call.

I didn't notice that line two, which happened to be the last line I'd used, was blinking; it didn't occur to me that Bess might be using Julian's phone. I overheard her say, "—still have your business card, and may need your help after all."

I hung up quietly and punched the button for another line. I wasn't able to reach my friend, but I spent an hour or so proofing my trial brief and making up voir dire questions for my jury trial. I could hear Bess pacing around Julian's office, so I knew she hadn't gone home. When I was ready to call it a night, I went out the fire exit to avoid passing Julian's office.

I went home, took my ringing telephone off the hook, got stoned, showered, and changed my clothes. Then I walked the three blocks to my parents' flat, and fidgeted through Daddy's welcome-home dinner, waiting to get him alone so I could find out where the hell he'd been for two weeks. Mother spent the whole time complaining about the "gestapo grilling" to which Surgelato's henchmen had subjected her.

Over dessert, when Mother was finally running out of steam, Surgelato himself showed up.

Mother immediately lay down on the floor.

Surgelato glanced down. "I'm not here for you, Ms. Jansson. I'd like a word with your daughter."

I lay down, too.

"Funny," he commented, offering me his hand. "You were out of your office from some time before two o'clock until some time past five-thirty."

I got to my feet. "I had a hearing. Were you looking for me?"

"We found several telephone messages on your desk. One in your garbage. Time on it was five-thirty. Presumably you returned to your office and—"

"Is something the matter, Lieutenant?" Daddy had come up behind me, his hands reassuringly on my shoulders.

"Why were you going through my garbage?"

Surgelato's face was expressionless. His black hair was as

untidy as its length would allow. He concentrated on me, ignoring my father. "What time did you leave your office for home—or wherever—today?"

"Around quarter to seven; I don't know. I got back from my hearing a little after six. I returned a call; I did some paperwork."

"Was anybody else in the office when you arrived there shortly after six o'clock?"

"If you were searching without a warrant, then some kind of a felony must have—"

"Was anybody else—?"

"Bess Warneke. She was in Julian's office."

Surgelato's jaw clamped. "How did you ascertain that Mrs. Warneke was—?"

"I walked by Julian's office and the door was open. I saw Bess in there."

"Did she attempt to explain her presence?"

He didn't usually talk that way; it was spooky, like watching *Dragnet* in 3-D. "She was crying. I don't think she even saw me. I walked right past—" I heard my voice fade. I reached out and clutched the lieutenant's jacket, a tight gray plaid. "What happened? She's all right, isn't she?"

Surgelato frowned at the hand I'd attached to his lapel. He said, "Come with me, please. We believe you possess material information in regard to a capital crime, and—"

I heard my mother moan.

"Capital—! What's happened to Bess?" I could feel my father's hands slide under my elbows to support me.

But, "Please come with me," was all Surgelato would say.

• CHAPTER ELEVEN •

I hate men. When things go wrong for them, they get surly. Okay, so Surgelato was under a lot of pressure. A prominent lawyer had been murdered; so, I gathered, had his ex-wife. Local papers had been harping on the law school murders and blaming Surgelato and the D.A. for the voluntary-man-slaughter verdict. An oft-quoted columnist had quipped, "Give the lieutenant enough rope and he'll let the murderer hang everyone in sight."

It wasn't pleasant for me, either, but I didn't get crabby and polysyllabic with Surgelato.

Anyway, he took me back to the law office. A huge notice was stapled to the door: POLICE BUSINESS ONLY. KEEP OUT. Every light in the place was on, and men in blue uniforms cluttered the reception room, upending wastebaskets and moving chairs. Surgelato talked briefly to a man in a sloppy suit, then led me to Julian's office. A man with two cameras and a leather backpack blocked the doorway. He was explaining to someone inside how to photograph praying mantises. He moved aside without interrupting his disser-tation.

Surgelato let me step into the room and see for myself what had happened. It didn't appear to trouble him that Bess had been an acquaintance of mine. I wondered if he was counting on my falling to pieces.

I made it a point not to, though it took some doing.

Bess sat at Julian's desk, hunched over her handbag. Her

forehead rested on the desk blotter. Her scarf appeared singed above one ear. Paper bags covered her hands, tied at the wrist with package twine. A man squatted beside her, applying white powder to the arm of Julian's leather chair. He used something that looked like a makeup brush. I could hear muffled conversation in Julian's bathroom.

The lieutenant asked me curtly, "This where you last saw her?"

The paper bags over Bess's hands seemed the most gruesome part of the tableau, somehow; maybe because I didn't understand their function. "Yes. Right there. Right where she is now."

"She was definitely alive?"

"Yes. She came out of the bathroom and put the key back in Julian's desk. She was crying."

"But you didn't speak to her?"

"No."

"Why not?"

"I told you—she was crying." I stared at the paper bags. Had something happened to her hands? "I didn't want to bother her. I went right to my office."

"And she didn't speak to you?"

"She didn't see me." The room stank of emptied bladder. It strained my pretense of nonchalance.

"So she didn't know you were here?"

"I made a phone call from my office. She might have seen the light on Julian's telephone. I used line one. She was on line two."

"So Mrs. Warneke made a call? You saw her talking—?"

"No, I didn't see her. I picked up the phone in my office, and Bess was on the line. She was saying, 'I've got your card and I need your help'; something like that." From Julian's bathroom came the sound of laughter. "What happened to her?"

"Bullet in the temple."

"Suicide?" I extended a shaky hand toward the wall, but Surgelato intercepted it. Fingerprints, I guess.

"Possibly. A couple of things don't satisfy us." He watched me, taking an extra second to release my hand. "You hear anyone else come into this office?"

"I heard Bess pacing around."

"You know for a fact it was her?"

I considered this. "Unless Bess opened the reception room door, no one else could have gotten in. The door was locked when I got here, and I left it locked."

Surgelato trod gingerly toward the desk. He watched the crouching man apply a wide strip of tape to the powdered chair arm. "You've heard of keys, I guess, Miss Jansson." He kept his eyes on the fingerprint man.

"No, nobody at this firm would have hurt Bess. We all liked her. She mixed . . ."

He turned to face me. "Yes?"

"Great drinks; but I guess that's irrelevant. Do you think—? There's a window in Julian's bathroom."

"Human fly?" He turned back to the crouching man. "Was Mrs. Warneke still sitting here when you left to go home?"

"Well . . . actually, I went out the back way. Through the fire exit."

Even the crouching man stopped working to look at me. Surgelato's small eyes narrowed beneath his missing-link browbone. "And why the hell did you do that?"

"I didn't want Bess to see me. You know, and have to act cheerful."

The lieutenant is a short, broad man who puffs himself up like a lizard to look scary. It works, too. "So for all you know, there could have been ten people in this office when you left."

"Ten people wouldn't fit."

He waved his hand in a gesture that made it plain he'd

been raised by Italians. "Okay: why I brought you here. Look around the office: You see anything out of place? Anything that shouldn't be here? That should be here but isn't?"

I looked at the desk first and quickly, trying not to focus on Bess. No one had gotten around to packing up Julian's belongings yet. His dandelion-in-glass paperweight was still there, his pen set, his yellow Post-its, some legal pads, a mug. Mae Siegel had removed his client files, so the desk might have looked uncluttered but for Bess, sprawled over it.

"What are the paper bags for?"

"Preserve trace evidence on the hands. Keep looking. How about the walls?"

Pastel chalk drawings of Mexican peasants in fields adorned two walls, as they had since the midseventies, when Julian had insisted on dropping Teamster clients who competed with Cesar Chavez's Farmworkers of America. Clement Kerrey, I heard, had defended the Teamsters' right to organize farmworkers. He'd predicted Chavez would grow inaccessible and autocratic without the competition. When his prediction had proved correct, Clement had made a point of bringing boycotted grapes to law firm potlucks. Julian had invariably thrown them away.

The third wall of Julian's office was taken up by a row of narrow windows. The fourth was covered with photographs in cheap black frames. I walked over to them. They showed Julian with such left-wing luminaries as Jane Fonda, Aaron Bancroft, Harvey Milk, Jerry Brown, Angela Davis, Alan Cranston, Jerry Rubin, Silvio Bernstein, Jesse Jackson, and (I don't know why) Andy Warhol. I looked at the pictures for a long time.

"There might have been more."

Surgelato bounded over. "Where?"

I pointed to two small nail holes at one end.

"What was up here? Remember?"

"This looks like all of them, but— I don't know. Part of my brain says something's gone."

Surgelato shifted one of the photographs to expose a darker square of unfaded wallpaper behind it. Whatever had hung from the missing nails had obviously been removed before the paper faded. The lieutenant shrugged.

I turned my attention to the rest of the office. I looked at the love seat and ottoman in the corner, at the library table with the green-shaded banker's lamp, at the books stacked on the floor. Without Julian's case files, the place seemed unusually tidy, but nothing else struck me. I told Surgelato so.

He bellowed, "Krisbaum!"

The sloppy-suited man waddled through the door.

"Take her to an empty office and babysit her till I'm done here."

Krisbaum grinned, motioning for me to precede him down the hall.

Habit took me to my own office. I flung open the door, and a disgruntled-looking plainclothesman leaped to his feet, waving me out.

But I hardly noticed him. Sitting opposite him at *my* desk, drinking out of *my* coffee cup, was Edward goddam Hershey!

In a frenzy of outrage, I shouted, "That's *my* cup!"

Edward Hershey glanced at the cup, then set it down abruptly, saying, "Jesus, I might catch something!"

Krisbaum tugged me back into the corridor. He tried to steer me toward Felix's office, but I shoved him aside. I didn't get a chance to tell Edward what I thought of his joke, though; the disgruntled plainclothesman slammed the door in my face.

I wheeled on Krisbaum. "What's *he* doing in my office?"

"Ask the lieutenant. And let's not get physical, do you mind?"

I fumed for five or ten minutes, pacing around Felix

Flish's office while Krisbaum flipped through computer magazines. *Might catch something*: very fucking funny.

Surgelato didn't know what he was walking into; the moment he entered, I exploded. I'm not sure what all I said, but my voice seemed about an octave higher than usual.

Finally, Surgelato cut in. "Hershey's the one who phoned us; that's why he's here. If you don't want him drinking out of your cup—"

"*He* called you? What do you mean, *he*—?"

"Picked up the telephone and dialed our number. Said he was supposed to meet Mrs. Warneke here, but she didn't answer when he knocked. Said the door was locked, so he got the janitor to open—"

"The janitor wouldn't let *him* in here!"

"They found Mrs. Warneke—"

"And why would Bess phone *him*? He's lying!"

"Jeez—remind me never to borrow your coffee cup!" Surgelato nodded Krisbaum out of the room. "You say you heard Mrs. Warneke talking on the phone?" He dropped into a chair, glancing idly at Felix's computer terminal, at the framed Stanford Law diploma on the wall above it.

"Bess didn't even know Edward! He introduced himself to her at Julian's wake! So why would she phone—?" I remembered Edward handing Bess his business card at the wake. "I still have your card," Bess had said on the phone.

Surgelato watched me. "Hershey introduced himself at Warneke's wake?"

"What? Yes. At the wake. What does he do, anyway? What's his business?"

"I thought you knew him. Or do you just hate strangers drinking out of your—?"

"I met him years ago in Boston. Then he came out here to go to Cal. What does he do now?"

"You heard Mrs. Warneke say she still had someone's card. Is that right?"

I nodded.

"Did you happen to notice whether Hershey gave—"

"Yes, he gave her his card. What does he do?"

"You actually saw her look at it? She didn't just toss it?"

"She read it. What does he do?"

Surgelato mouthed the word "shit!" without actually saying it. "He's a private investigator."

"A private—!" I couldn't help myself; Edward bombs-guns-and-a-general-strike Hershey. A detective.

"You find that humorous?"

I wiped my eyes. "Somewhere between ironic and ridiculous."

"Why ironic?"

"He used to be Mr. Off-the-pigs."

There was a flicker of some baser emotion in Surgelato's eyes. "Charming. How did you meet him?"

"At a meeting. Socialist Workers Party."

Surgelato stifled a derisive snicker. "You became—good friends?"

"As they say in the tabloids."

"You *parted* friends?"

"We parted."

Being in the middle of North Beach hadn't prevented me from punching Edward in the nose. A nun, crossing Washington Square to Peter and Paul's Cathedral, had had to pull me off him.

"But you saw him again?"

"Not until Julian's wake. He's really a private eye?"

"He carries a photostat of a license. We're checking it out."

"So Bess wanted to hire a private eye." I felt a prickle of morbid interest. If only she'd called someone I could talk to. Anyone but Edward.

"Krisbaum'll take you to the Hall and get your statement." Surgelato frowned till his brows met his lashes. "Wasn't that long ago you made a lot of extra work for me. I didn't like it; you hear what I'm saying?"

I guess my morbid interest showed.

• CHAPTER TWELVE •

My father lay on my couch, watching me smoke a joint. He said mildly, "You're getting into a bad relationship with marijuana, Willa."

I considered stretching out on the floor. Yesterday's microwave pouches were a few inches from my left hand, baking in the afternoon sun and trapping dustballs; I decided to scale a chair instead. "Weren't we supposed to have this conversation twenty years ago?" I dropped the joint into a gummy ashtray. "Besides, I can't quit in the middle of Reagan's antidrug crusade!"

Daddy smiled. "I suppose not."

"So where have you been?"

He sighed, closing his eyes and rubbing his pale gold hair with his wrist. "Nicaragua?" he ventured.

"Not unless Silvio Bernstein can be two places at once."

He opened his eyes again; there was a twinkle of amusement in them. "You talked to Silvio?"

"Yes. He assumes you've got a floozy stashed away somewhere."

"Just the opposite, I'm afraid."

"I'm too stoned to do opposites. What does that work out to?"

"Your mother."

I looked at Daddy. He was pale, almost gaunt, his translucent skin falling into hollows beneath his cheekbones, crinkles standing out around his eyes. "What about Mother?"

"I was all set to go with Silvio and he postponed the trip. Before I got a chance to tell your mother, I saw her at Caffè Roma." He frowned. "With somebody."

"Who?"

"I think I won't say who." He reached across my water-spotted coffee table and patted my hand. "I have my reasons, Willa. You'll respect that."

Actually, I didn't. But it was clear I wouldn't find out from Daddy, not if he was going to take that tone. "You thought the man was her lover?"

He nodded. "Psychosynthesis." Psychosynthesis was a favorite concept of my father's—that subconscious information could suddenly integrate itself into a conscious insight. "I can't really say any more without telling you who it was."

"What did you do?"

"Went home and waited. Your mother came in." He rubbed his eyes with a lightly freckled hand. "She talked about my trip in such a way that I thought it would be better if I pretended to go."

"So you could watch the house and catch them—?"

He smiled. "So I could give your mother space."

This was another favorite concept of my father's; growing up, I'd been given so much space that I'd practically gone into orbit. Disgusted, I went into the kitchen to boil water for his tea.

I stood at the sink letting water overflow the kettle. Daddy was cerebral enough to embrace most forms of altruism, but this . . . I considered myself fairly altruistic, and I'd all but degendered my last boyfriend for what he'd called "an inconsequential little interlude. Or two."

Daddy came through the swinging door and turned off the water for me. Then he crossed to the cupboard and began rooting behind half-empty cereal boxes for the teapot.

I set the kettle on the stove. "Where did you go? What did you do for two weeks?"

He made a show of pulling down all my boxes of tea, looking at the ingredients, smelling them. Finally he said, "Santa Cruz, Monterey, Big Sur."

"Did you go to the monastery?"

He nodded, selecting ginseng. "For a while, till I got tired of the peace and quiet."

"How's Brother Blaise?"

"Healthy as a horse."

I lit the gas burner. Good Brother Blaise had shucked his frock and moved to Castro Street, where I'd recently seen him in frocks of livelier hue.

I looked up to find Daddy grinning at me. "Did you say Brother Blaise? He's not there anymore. I was thinking of that other one—the one with the tonsure."

He'd guessed what I was up to. "Oh, *that* one."

Daddy turned away quickly, before our understanding became covert. "He sends you his best."

• CHAPTER THIRTEEN •

I interrupted Mother's alternate-nostril breathing. "What a thing to do to my *sati*!" she complained. "Is Daddy with you?"

"He stopped down to see Ben. A quick drink before Armageddon."

She de-lotused her legs, rubbing her ankles. "I can't·stop thinking about Bess."

"That can't be doing much for your *sati*."

"Such an unattractive quality, Baby! I think you'd even joke about—about—"

"About my own mother forging a will?"

She tsked. "Have you been smoking marijuana?"

"What is it with the marijuana? Next thing I know you guys'll be handing me a paper cup with my name on it—"

"These inappropriate remarks—"

"Are not drug·induced. You know Felix Flish, don't you?"

"Flish. Warneke da da da and Flish. He's in your law firm."

"You win the Tourister luggage. Do you know him? Personally?"

Slowly, she tilted her head toward her left shoulder, then her right. "I don't think so."

"Weren't you talking to someone called Felix on the phone last night?"

"No."

That's all, just "no." No crabbing about why was I bothering her with stupid questions and upsetting her *sati* and talking about Julian's will in that way of mine. Just "no."

I extended a hand to help her up. Her skin felt hot, waxy. "Mother, please tell me about it. I'll try to fix it so it doesn't backfire on you."

Her eyes grew wide, her mouth slack.

"Mother, I'm bound to find out anyway. And in the meantime, you might get into trouble I could have gotten you out of."

She jerked her hand out of mine, displaying much yogic straightness of spine. "I haven't done anything I'm ashamed of! And that's all I'm going to say about it!" She stalked off to her bedroom, slamming the door behind her.

I walked home along Haight Street, past boutiques that sold African masks, expensive teddy bears, espresso makers, and glittering tube tops (as if it were ever warm enough for them in San Francisco). Their windows were accordioned over with padlocked grilles. I remembered stores that stayed open until midnight, stores that sold licorice- and strawberry-flavored cigarette papers, and even, at times, something to roll into them.

I stopped to look at some mannequins with multicolored wigs and silver smears of face paint. Pinned to their outsized jackets were dozens of peace symbols. These days, teenagers wore them for the same reason they wore ducktails and studded leather: no reason.

My reflection in the streaked window looked windblown and cranky. Julian eating hemlock root with his amaretto mousse, Jim Zissner's car going over Devil's Slide, Bess Warneke crying—then dying—in Julian's office. Either it was too much for my brain to psychosynthesize or Daddy was right about me smoking too much pot.

And Edward fucking Hershey a detective.

The thought of him sticking his arrogant nose into things

nearly made me shriek with irritation. My boss had been murdered, and my parents were involved, somehow; I could feel it. I might be able to shield them; Edward wouldn't give a damn.

Might catch something! Stupid bastard.

I hadn't done too badly in the detecting department myself, back in law school. I'd complicated things for Surgelato, but I'd been right about a lot of things, too.

I'd show Edward Hershey a thing or two.

• CHAPTER FOURTEEN •

When I was seven years old, Lissa TreeSky, candlemaker and sole proprietor of the Haight Street Alternative School, tried to interest me in books like *Sharp Ears, the Baby Whale* and *Luis of Guadalajara*. But in keeping with the spirit of alternative education, Lissa was reluctant to ram the books down my throat. Instead she'd sit on the floor, her waist-length hair spilling onto the pages as she quietly read them aloud. Instead of listening to long passages about how to grind corn for tortillas or weave dead grass into sombreros, I devoured books like *The Clue of the Twisted Candle*. Lissa usually continued reading until my classmate—who was hyperactive in spite of Lissa's experiments with yin-yang ratios in his diet—began hurling dolls at her (Lissa did not allow us to play with "violent" toys like guns).

I did ultimately read *Sharp Ears*; it's about the migration of a baby whale. It would take a *heavily* yang diet to make it seem exciting; and it certainly doesn't hold a twisted candle to Nancy Drew. Maybe Lissa realized this; she finally took a different tack. She explained to me that Nancy Drew was an upper-class Philistine, that her father was one of the Bosses, and that their housekeeper, Hannah, engaged in white Uncle Tom-ism. That's when I gave *Sharp Ears* a try—and decided I preferred to live with Nancy's political shortcomings.

Since Lissa did not want to impose a "rigid curriculum" on us, I spent most of what should have been third and fourth grades reading Nancy Drew, Judy Bolton, Trixie Belden, and (much to Lissa's horror) Annette Funicello mysteries. I still can't multiply or divide or do many of the other things fourth graders are taught to do. But I do know a good mystery when I see it.

So instead of returning Matthilde Warneke's phone call, I went to see her.

From the outside, Julian Warneke's (soon to be my mother's) house was a picture of understated elegance: two story with a gray stucco exterior and white trim, including molded plaster ribbons along the roof and between the floors. One wall abutted an overadorned Victorian, and the other a shingled three story with stained glass windows. Six-foot trees lined both sides of the street, and a short block to my left, joggers did knee bends on the grass strip separating the bay from the street. However my mother had accomplished it, I had to give her credit: it was a step up from a two-bedroom flat in the Haight.

Matthilde, wearing jeans, an L. L. Bean sweater, and wooden clogs, opened the door. "You didn't return my call yesterday," she pouted.

"It was late when I got back to the office."

She led me into the living room, gesturing at the bare walls and corners. "Bess took all the antiques. The court said Julian was entitled to some of them, but Bess took them anyway. Most of what's here is my old stuff." Her color was high, her expression enervated. "I can't *believe* I used to admire that woman!"

It seemed a cold-blooded statement, under the circumstances.

I looked around the room. A monastery-style couch, table, and love seat. Cluttered built-in bookcases. Photo albums spread on the uncarpeted oak floor: photographs and old newspaper clippings about Julian. But no television and no morning paper.

Matthilde pointed to the albums. "I've started a book

about him. I've got a lot of original source material." She frowned. "I wish his kids would let me have some of their pictures and letters."

My impulse was to make an excuse and leave. "You haven't heard yet, have you?"

"About your mother?" She twisted her long black hair into a coil at the base of her neck and tucked it down the back of her sweater. "I don't understand why Julian would— His family's bound to sue her. I haven't decided yet if I'm—"

"Bess is dead."

Matthilde shook her head. "No she isn't."

"She went to Julian's office last night and either she killed herself or someone shot her."

Matthilde took a few steps backward. She misjudged the proximity of the couch and sat down too soon, hitting the wooden edge hard enough to send a hell of a shock up her tailbone. She didn't even wince. "Are you joking?"

My sense of humor may be morbid, but I found her question a little insulting. "No. Bess is dead. It's in the papers."

She continued to stare. "Killed herself?"

"Or somebody shot her. The police don't know."

She gaped at the photo albums spread on the floor. Judging from her expression, she was doing some serious psychosynthesizing. I wondered what kind of insight could be garnered from Bess's death and a floor full of old photographs.

Curious, I knelt in front of them. There were a couple of dozen pictures scattered over the photo album pages. Julian as a black-haired young man with a crafty expression; Julian and Bess, thin and well dressed, with their kids; Julian at rallies; Julian embracing clients; Julian with other lawyers, most frequently his bearded and bespectacled former partner Martin Rittenhaus. I couldn't remember having seen any of the pictures on the wall of Julian's office.

One photo did strike a chord, though. Martin Rittenhaus, towering over Julian and twenty years his junior, was leaning forward to say something to a wild-haired Aaron Bancroft. At Aaron's feet was a picket sign that read Vietnam Is None Of Our Business. Julian and Rittenhaus wore suits with loosened ties, and Aaron wore a tie-dyed T-shirt. They and the crowd behind them stood beneath a sign that read Dow Chemical. There was something familiar about the scene—not the photo, but the scene. I wondered if I'd been to that rally.

I looked up to find Matthilde standing over me, her nostrils flared and her lips pinched. I stood up, too. "I thought you knew about Bess. I'm sorry to bring you bad news."

Matthilde knelt gracefully, gathering up the photo albums. In the diffuse light of a sheered window, she looked as gauzily beautiful as Loretta Young.

She carried the albums to the couch, where she kept a proprietary hand on them. "I heard about Jim Zissner." There was a hint of defensiveness in her tone, as if knowing about Zissner made up for not knowing about Bess. "Julian didn't like him."

I guess Julian had lost his taste for radical hotheads when he'd acquired a taste for sorbet between courses.

Matthilde looked away. "I was thinking about it. Thinking about everyone who had lunch with Julian that day. I went out to dinner—" Her expression grew more cheerful, she looked me in the eye again. "With Bill Ingram, in fact. We talked about you."

I felt like slapping her. They'd talked about me when they'd been lovers, too; Matthilde had suggested I try the new herpes drug, Acyclovir. "How is Bill?"

"Fine. He works out; he's got a great tan. He lives down in L.A., in-house counsel for one of the studios."

"The world gone mad," I muttered.

"What?"

"I'm glad."

"I noticed our garnishes, the orange slices and parsley, were on the left side of the plate."

I shook my head, wondering what difference it made where her parsley had been.

She leaned closer, blinking her big eyes at me. "Someone told me Clement was sitting on Julian's left."

Ah. "And you think Clement put the hemlock on Julian's mousse. I'm sure the police have considered—"

"You know that lieutenant, don't you? From law school, when all those editors were—?"

"Yes."

"Willa, do you trust Clement?"

"Sure. I mean, I've never really thought about it."

"Because I'm sure Julian wanted Felix to get something! That horse he left Clement. Or *something*! They were so close!"

I was surprised to hear her say so. I'd gotten the impression *she* was the one who'd been "close" to Felix.

"Felix was over here all the time!" She blushed. "And Julian used to say he'd guaranteed Felix's future."

"What do you mean, 'guaranteed'?"

"I thought he meant in his will. I was surprised when they read it. That he'd leave that racehorse to Clement and all that wine to Brian and nothing to Felix."

"Maybe he meant making Felix a partner. Putting him above Clement and Brian's whims."

Or maybe Julian had left his house to my mother, with *instructions*.

"There's something wrong with Clement, Willa! I can feel it! I'm sensitive to that kind of vibration! Do you know how much that horse is worth?"

"No."

"It might be worth a lot of money." She flipped her hair back out from under her sweater. I noticed her hand was trembling. "I thought since you knew the lieutenant . . ."

I waited for her to finish the thought. She didn't. "You want me to find out how much the horse is worth?"

She slid the top photo album off the stack and put it on her knee. "No. I thought you could tell him—if you think it's a good idea—about their problems, Julian and Clement's."

"What problems?"

She reached into the album and pulled out an envelope. She handed it to me.

It contained a draft of a legal document. An offer from Julian to buy Clement Kerrey's partnership share in the closed legal corporation of Warneke, Kerrey, Lieberman & Flish. I was shocked; it was like finding out Donder wanted to buy out Blitzen.

Matthilde leaned forward on the couch. Her hair smelled of sweet herbs. "I found it with Julian's papers. I don't know if Clement knew about it or not."

"You didn't tell Surgelato?"

Matthilde shook her head.

I read it more carefully. It offered "my friend and partner Clem Kerrey" the fair market value of his one partnership share. The document also guaranteed Clement the right to take with him any client. In smooth red felt-tip, Julian had modified this to read, "any client for whom he has principal litigation responsibility, if that client so chooses." Julian had scribbled a few other revisions in the margins, but it seemed a fair-enough offer on its face.

"Look, Matthilde, if Clement didn't know about this, there's no point in showing it to the police. And if he did know, then it's his responsibility to say something—and his right not to." I tucked the document into its envelope and handed it back. She seemed disappointed. "Just because partners get on each other's nerves, or whatever the problem was, it doesn't mean they'd murder each other. And the offer's fair. It lets Clement keep his labor clients."

"But it gives him all the overhead of running his own office! And the labor part of- the practice *loses* money!"

"It does?"

Matthilde nodded. "Teamsters are so cheap! Julian complained about it all the time."

• CHAPTER FIFTEEN •

My landlord, Ben Bubniak, was talking to reporters in his "store," a garage wherein he offered Rosicrucian secrets, Gurdjieff books, used sci-fi comics, alien-being posters, Lyndon LaRouche pamphlets about the Trilateral Commission, and Jehovah's Witness tracts about the New Jerusalem. Whatever Ben was telling the reporters (I could see his grand gestures through the raised garage door), he had their full attention; they didn't notice me skulking into the building.

Someone else did, though. When I tried to slam the door shut, it rebounded off Edward fucking Hershey's foot. It caught me in the back, almost knocking me to the floor. When I saw who it was, I repeatedly thumped the door against the toe of his boot. I believe I was swearing.

"Give me a break, Willa." Hershey grabbed the door knob. "I'm just trying to do my job."

He wedged his shoulder against one side of the door and I wedged mine against the other, and we both pushed. He grunted, "Do I have to sic another nun on you?"

He won the shoving match, even without the nun. He took a step into the room, pushing back the hair that hung untidily over his forehead. "Come on, Willa. I just want to talk to you for a minute. I don't like finding my clients dead." He inclined his head slightly. "Makes it hard to collect my fee."

"I wouldn't tell you anything if—"

"Your life depended on it?" He cast disparaging glances

at my cheap teak and futons. "What if someone else's life depends on it?"

"Why would Bess Warneke hire *you*?"

"I happen to be a good shamus."

"So good you have to hand out business cards at funerals!"

A half smile. "I'm not above a little hearse chasing. You want to trade information?"

"Do you know anything I want to know?"

He nodded. "A couple of things Bess Warneke said on the phone. You tell me what went on in Warneke's office last night, and I'll tell you what Mrs. Warneke said."

It's hard, wanting somthing from someone you loathe. Especially someone you've loathed for a long time. Between warnings and precautions, Edward Hershey had cost me a lot of foreplay, a lot of pride, and a lot of reputation.

"Tell you what, W. J.: I'll even go first."

Considering nothing had happened in the office (nothing I knew about, anyway), it was a difficult offer to refuse. "You first?"

"Deal. What is this thing, anyway? Do I sit on it?"

"It's a futon."

He sank into it, grinning up at me. "I'd rather not get a crick in my neck."

I sat on the coffee table.

"Okay, six-fourteen yesterday, I get a call from Mrs. Warneke. She says she's at Julian's office. She says she thinks with a little help she can blow Julian's will out of the water. That she's got some 'proof.' That she owes it to her kids." He tapped my foot with his boot. "Who gets Warneke's dough if the will's invalidated? Kids?"

I was reluctant to answer; I didn't want to speak to the bastard. But I supposed he might have more to tell me. I made sure my tone was suitably grudging. "They'd get his separate property. Matthilde Warneke would get his community property."

"That's pretty much what I figured."

"No doubt." It was characteristic of Hershey to pretend he knew everything.

"Major bequest is that house of his. That'd be separate property, right? He bought it before he married the new Mrs. W."

I nodded.

"So I tell her it'll take me two hours to drive up from Santa Cruz, but she says she'll wait. To come ASAP to Warneke's office." He sat forward on the futon, collapsing the edge and sinking into a semisupported squat. "But nobody answers when I knock. So I get the janitor; we go in there," he paused for effect, "and there she is holding a twenty-two automatic. Hole in her temple, scarf melted into her hair. And not a clue what her 'proof' is." He scowled. "Your mother inherits Warneke's house, doesn't she?"

"Your story's bullshit. You just need an excuse for being at the scene of the crime."

"Ah." He lounged against the futon back. "So I make up a phony reason for Bess Warneke to hire a detective. Except that the phone company keeps records of long distance calls, and I can prove Mrs. Warneke phoned my office."

"You can prove *someone* phoned your office from our office. But you could have done that yourself."

He nodded. "Yeah, I suppose." Again he tapped my moccasin with the toe of his boot. "But the cops tell me you overheard Mrs. Warneke say she needed my help."

"I overheard her say she needed *somebody's* help."

"Whatever," he said cheerfully. "Your turn. What exactly *did* Mrs. Warneke tell you?"

With equal good cheer, I replied, "Not a goddam thing. I didn't talk to her."

"But you were at the office—cops told me you were."

"I was, but I didn't talk to her. Not a word. I saw her in Julian's office, but she didn't see me."

Hershey squinted at me. "And you didn't even say 'hello, ma'am'?"

I shook my head.

"Give me a fucking break! I'm not—"

I never found out what Hershey wasn't.

A two-hundred-pound slab of police detective chose that moment to knock at my door.

• CHAPTER SIXTEEN •

It's not enough, apparently, to spend five hours answering every moronic question the police brain can devise. It is also necessary to cross town the next day and dictate a statement to a semiliterate officer so that he can slump over a typewriter like a befuddled chimpanzee and type it—slowly, slowly—with two bratwurstlike fingers. When he finally presents you with the resulting mass of typos, you are supposed to sign it—you are not supposed to point out the numerous misspellings. If you do point them out, in fact, the policeman will leave you in a tiny, crowded anteroom to be jostled by reporters and snickered at by passing cops. An hour and a half later, if you are lucky, the policeman may give you another chance to sign the same, uncorrected statement.

I'd been through the routine before. The only good thing about it, this day, was that the cop had spirited me away from Edward lying Hershey.

I got back home in time to find Ben closing his shop.

"Mailman couldn't fit all this into your box." He handed me a sheaf of letters.

Hate mail. I'd gotten some after the law school murders (most of it in two categories: The-more-lawyers-murdered-the-better and Who-do-you-think-you're-kidding-everybody-knows-*you*-did-it). San Francisco being what it is, I'd expected more of the same after Julian's murder. Still, the vitriol of anonymous cranks disturbed me; I didn't need reminding that the city teemed with crazies.

71

"What were you telling those reporters, Ben?"

"About the nose cone."

"They must have loved that story." Ben and my parents and a defrocked priest had hammered a few dents into a missile nose cone in 1974. The Berrigans had done the same thing a couple of months later. At that rate, every missile in America would sport a scratch or two by the year 5500. ("It's the *symbolism* of the thing!" Mother had insisted when I'd visited her at the San Bruno jail. "You've never appreciated *symbolism*!")

"And let's see, the blood on the draft files back in sixty-nine. Or was it seventy? When did you get back from Boston, Earth Woman?"

"Seventy-one. I thought Martin Rittenhaus represented you guys on that one."

"One of the reporters, kind of a quiet fellow from the *Chronicle*, asked about Rittenhaus."

I dropped my mail. "Tall and skinny, dark complexion, and sort of a pointy nose? Pauses before he asks questions?"

Ben nodded.

"Manuel Boyd. Why was he asking about Rittenhaus?"

"Boyd—I remember. He used to work for one of those free papers. Covered your murder case, didn't he? Wrote a piece about that wino of yours."

"Boyd's not your average reporter, that's for damned sure. Did he try to come upstairs and see me? He called my office yesterday—"

"Whole crew of them saw that cop stick you into his car."

"I wonder if it's just coincidence that Bill Ingram's in town. The guy who made the movie about Rittenhaus."

"Rittenhaus is a lot more famous than Julian, god bless him. Brilliant man, Rittenhaus was. Maybe not as *ideological* as Julian, but . . ." Ben shrugged forgivingly.

After they poured blood on draft files, Rittenhaus cajoled

Ben and my parents into pleading guilty to trespassing in exchange for dismissal of the other charges. It was a testament to Rittenhaus's brilliance that he'd gotten them suspended sentences—and still retained their respect.

Ben patted his pockets, extracting from one the latest pamphlet to emerge from his "desktop publisher."

I skimmed it as I phoned Matthilde Warneke. It was about Ronald Reagan's pact with the devil, and it was the best explanation I've ever read for the man's popularity with Congress and the electorate.

"Bill Ingram's at the Mark Hopkins," Matthilde informed me, in answer to my question. "He'll be glad to hear from you, Willa. He always thought you resented—"

I quickly hung up. My phone rang the minute I replaced the receiver. Reporters in a fact-finding frenzy, no doubt. I didn't answer. I went to the Mark.

I hadn't seen Bill Ingram since our civil procedure final, five years earlier; the following quarter he'd transferred to UCLA. I remembered him as untidy, slouched, and unshorn. So I was surprised to see him wearing pleated white slacks, a pressed purple shirt, an indigo tie and gray kid shoes. He stood very straight, and when he embraced me I noticed the effect of bench presses, curls, and other unnatural acts. Most shocking of all, his hair looked like something from a John Davidson wig boutique.

And me in my saggy sweater and threadbare jeans (thank goodness I'd had my moccasins rebeaded). "You look good," I lied, stepping into his suite.

"So do you," he lied back.

"Been here long?"

"About three weeks. Oakland's suing the studio over some things that went wrong when we filmed on location here last year. Can you believe it? We should sue *them* for being so god-awful ugly."

Three weeks. Long enough.

Bill picked up the phone, gave his room number, and requested "Dom for two. Not too cold."

"You heard about Julian Warneke? You saw Matthilde, so you must have heard."

Bill sat beside me on an imitation Louis XIV love seat, slipping his arm behind the carved rose back. "*Quel* bummer! I didn't always agree with Warneke's ideas, but—"

"You didn't?"

His eyelids drooped and his lips curled. "I'm a peripheralist, myself."

He was certainly marginal, but I doubted that's what he meant. "I'm not familiar with the term."

He seemed pleased. "A peripheralist is someone who believes that change in the law follows change in the society at large. Warneke believed you could change the law first, and thereby *force* social change."

"But that's obviously right. Look at the Civil Rights Act."

"It reflected existing change."

"In Mississippi? It *forced* change."

"No, no. I did my LL.M. thesis on the subject, if you'd care to see it."

"I'd love to." I'd read enough pompous tomes to last me a lifetime, editing a law review, but it seemed bad manners to say so. Instead I asked, "Did you get a chance to see Julian before he died?"

Bill Ingram's expression changed. Even his tone grew guarded. "No, I didn't look him up."

"Matthilde said you saw him."

It was a lie, but I'm not above lying; and I was well rewarded for my moral laxity. Ingram licked his lips and swallowed. A vein in his temple pulsed visibly.

"Did she?" he said.

I've had this trouble before, with lawyers. They won't lie outright, but neither will they volunteer a syllable of information. "I thought she did." I waited a beat or two; he still didn't volunteer information. "Did you find Julian changed from the Martin Rittenhaus days?"

"Old warhorses like Julian," he answered carefully, "never change. Listen, if this adversely affects your law firm dynamic, you should consider coming down to L.A. Entertainment law is *it*, Willa, I'm telling you!"

The "Dom" arrived (not too cold), and Bill spent the next half hour telling me what he must have supposed were amusing stories about movie stars he'd met. Thank god for the champagne.

I attempted once more to find out when he'd last seen Julian, but he put me off with a generous testimonial to the man (in spite of Julian's foolish refusal to embrace peripheralism). He did let one interesting fact slip: Matthilde Warneke was soon to be his guest in L.A. "So she can catch some rays and put the old guy behind her."

I left Bill's room gratefully. The champagne made me more than usually aware of the softness of the Mark's carpet, the dinnertray-carpet-cologne smell of the corridors, and the quiet glide of the elevator ride. I stood atop Nob Hill, within view of the Fairmont's flags, the gray stones of Grace Cathedral, the pillared facade of the Pacific Union Club, and the tranquil green lawn of Huntington Park. Behind me, the street plunged, rose slightly at the corner, plunged again—a descent that appeared to require rappelling skill.

I walked downhill. It was nearly dusk; headlights blinked on. Delis and theaters and ice cream shops and art galleries and health clubs glowed with interior light. The bay window of a three-story Victorian showcased two ruggedly handsome men touching wineglasses, then embracing. A white stretch limo passed a cable car, and the latter began ringing its bell. The air smelled of cool bay and, more faintly, of mingled Chinese and Italian food. I'd have given anything to walk all the way home on so perfect a night and in so good a mood. But between Nob

Hill and the Haight lay the Tenderloin, with its desperate drunks and prostitutes, and the Hayes Valley, with its acres of seething housing projects. I reckoned my chances of getting home—*with* my handbag—were about five percent. I stopped at a by-the-slice Sicilian-style pizza place, grabbed a bite, and called a cab.

There were two reporters sitting on the front steps of my building, so I told the cab driver to take me to my parents' flat.

I found Mother and Daddy serving herb tea to Clement Kerrey. If I hadn't already announced myself coming through the door, I'd have walked home and braved the reporters. Clement Kerrey and a snootful of good champagne didn't seem like a winning combination to me.

Clement wore a button-down shirt with an elbow-patched cardigan, corduroy slacks, and the ugliest of an ugly line of Hush Puppies. Whatever he and my parents were discussing, it was obviously of interest to him. He leaned forward on their cushionless canvas couch, his black eyes bright. He was stroking his beard, something he frequently did when thinking aloud.

The three of them looked at me, but only Daddy managed a smile.

"Am I interrupting?" I edged back toward the door. Clement wasn't exactly a frequent guest of my parents; funny he should show up the same day Matthilde had slandered him.

"Not at all." Clement smiled his broad, Mr. Love smile.

I was trapped. I went in, kissed Daddy's cheek, and sat cross-legged on the floor beside him. I waved to Mother, who was across the room on her *sati* pillow. "Did you hear any more about that Montara man?"

The peace-love smile vanished. "He's a Retail Clerk."

"Ah." The Teamsters and the Retail Clerks Union were locked in battle over several major retail chains. "That's good news, I suppose."

"We'll be slapping a slander suit on him and the Retail Clerks." Clement's nostrils flared.

"But don't you agree with Felix? That people only remember the bad things they read about the Teamsters, and not the good—"

"No, I don't agree with Felix! I don't agree with standing by while an antiunion press and a union-busting administration propagate lies—"

"But aren't you just feeding the fire? As long as the union's doing right by its members—"

"This false image hurts the union more than anything else! Every time they try to organize they come up against it! Management labor firms keep scrapbooks of unfavorable articles—"

"But Clement! You're talking about months of articles about so-and-so alleging. Management's not going to play fair and clip out that final tiny article announcing that the Teamsters won the lawsuit."

Clement compressed his lips. "Image is important to the union, and goddam it, I don't blame them a bit!" He glittered his eyes at me for a minute. "You need to see more of Semi and Hank and Pete and some of the others to understand what I'm saying. What's on your calendar next week?"

"Felix and Brian are divvying up Julian's cases and giving me some of theirs. So I'm not sure."

"Well, I'll tell you what. You leave Friday clear, and I'll take you to the joint council with me. Steve says you did fine on the Guiterrez pension case; I'll familiarize you with some of the other cases, and you can help me out next weekend." He smiled magnanimously, and I heard my mother make a pride-filled oohing noise.

The last thing on earth I wanted to do was spend a three-day weekend at Caesar's Tahoe with Semi Sawyer and his band of merry misogynists, but I said, "All right. Thank you."

When Clement left, I turned to Mother. "What was he doing here?"

"We're old friends," she said vaguely, handing Daddy her teacup so he could carry it into the kitchen with the others.

"You have lots of old friends. Why Clement? Why tonight? What were you talking about?"

From the kitchen, Daddy called out, "Julian's will."

Mother flushed. "We asked him how that new wife, the girl you went to school with—"

"You know her name, Mother."

"How she was fixed, and if we needed to worry about fairness. You know—with me getting the house." She brushed some imaginary crumbs off the mosaic-tile coffee table.

"Why would you expect Clement to know that?"

"Well, who else could I ask?"

"What did he say?"

"He said from what he knew of her, it would do her good to leave the nest and use her law degree. He didn't say it meanly, he spoke out of—"

"Love, I know."

"And really, with so few women having that kind of opportunity—"

"How much money *did* Julian leave Matthilde?"

"Clement doesn't think it's very much." Mother spoke apologetically. "Bess got most of it during their divorce to make up for Julian keeping the house."

"You know, I'm beginning to think Felix was right about Julian."

Maybe it was my imagination, but I thought Mother looked frightened. "What did he say?"

"That Julian was an old goat!"

She turned away, crossing herself.

• CHAPTER SEVENTEEN •

It seemed the longest car ride I'd ever endured. Six hours in a dinosaur of a Buick (Clement Kerrey would have been a Peugeot or a Volvo man, but for his determination to "buy American"). The first four hours were of flat road and empty landscape, with Clement talking about the joint council: which locals would be there, the types of workers they represented, whether they were having internal problems with the Teamsters for a Democratic Union.

"TDU doesn't see the blood, sweat, and tears that go into negotiating their damned contracts! They get pissed with the union over a few pennies an hour that Jesus Christ himself couldn't shake out of the employer. Or they get canned, and even after we waste the union's money grieving it, they say the union didn't do enough." Clement seemed wholly unaware of the road as we criss-crossed over both straight, flat lanes.

I held onto the armrest. "Like that waiter at René's?"

We missed an oncoming car by inches. I forced myself to stop looking out the window. I looked at Clement. He was frowning grimly, his knuckles white as he gripped the steering wheel.

I persisted. "Remember the waiter? The day Julian died? He was complaining about his union."

Clement nodded.

"Don't we represent the Hotel and Restaurant Workers Union?"

"René's is Teamster."

"Teamster? A restaurant?"

"They were trying to organize the delivery and janitorial people. Before the certification election, the employer got the employees' unit expanded to include kitchen and waiters, thinking they'd vote against the union." Clement smiled. "They didn't."

"So René's is part of Local 16?"

Clement nodded.

I looked out the window again. The scenery would have been a blur, had there been any scenery. "Did you order dessert that day, Clement?"

"I had the same as Julian."

"Did yours have a garnish in it?"

"I don't think so. I'm not sure. I didn't eat it, if it did."

"I suppose the police asked you about it."

"Oh, yes."

"Did you tell them about the waiter?"

"What about the waiter?"

"You were pretty snippy with him when he started complaining about his union. Do you suppose he might have—? I mean, if you and Julian ordered the same thing, maybe *you* were supposed to get Julian's."

He glanced at me and patted my hand. "How many people do you suppose eat their garnishes, Willa?" He shook his head. "A waiter could hardly count on it. No, unfortunately, it's more likely that whoever did it knew about Julian's habit."

In my mind's eye, I saw the document Julian Warneke had drawn up, booting Clement Kerrey out of the law firm.

• CHAPTER EIGHTEEN •

Caesar's Tahoe is gaudier than a bad acid trip. It has acres of red-and-gold carpet crowded with cocktail waitresses in mini togas, flushed gamblers in tight polyester, and bulgingly explicit "Roman" statues. Slot machines whir, keno boards flash, cigar smokers hack, Teamsters whoop, service bells clang, and a hundred conversations swell to a two-hundred-decibel roar. The stench of tobacco and alcohol permeates every inch of the place, including the bedding in each garish room.

My own room had the lobby's vile carpeting running halfway up the wall, where it was met by clashing flocked velvet wallpaper. The bedspread, in turn, clashed with both patterns, as did the shower curtain around the circular bathtub, which was, inexplicably, smack in the middle of the room. I won't even mention the curtains.

Clement told me to go ahead and do some gambling until that evening's banquet. But I don't gamble; I'm too pessimistic to believe I'll win anything. And even if I did gamble, I wouldn't do it in a room that might have been designed by Caligula.

So I went outside to try to find Lake Tahoe. I walked and walked, and what I finally found was a chain-link fence separating the town from the lake. The casinos weren't about to encourage any form of recreation other than gambling, I guess. At least the fence wasn't electrified.

I walked back along the neon nightmare of a main street,

wishing I were home. I had reached Caesar's parking lot when I saw someone I knew dashing into the hotel. I ran to catch up, but she'd already disappeared into the welter of people and smells and noises.

My secretary, Mae Siegel.

She hadn't been back to the office since Jim Zissner's death; she'd taken the week off. I doubted she'd come to Tahoe for the scenery. I had no idea why she'd come to the joint council, but whatever her reason, the secretary-treasurer of Local 16 wouldn't like it. With Teamster elections only a few weeks away, Semi Sawyer wouldn't like his dead—and very possibly murdered—opponent's lover haunting the council.

And what Semi Sawyer didn't like, Clement Kerrey didn't like, either.

• CHAPTER NINETEEN •

The Teamsters were in a camaraderous mood, and several of them knew "good old Willy and June" from some picket line or other. They accepted me—not as their lawyer, but as the daughter of two "friends of the working man." Clement was pleased to find me tossing down whiskey and sevens with "the boys," and I was having a pretty good time listening to their brush-with-death yarns. In the middle of one such tale, about a rig that overturned on a mountain road and seesawed on the edge of a cliff for "it musta been a good five minutes, fellas, I swear," I looked up and saw an old friend of mine skulking to the banquet room bar.

I excused myself and worked my way across the room to him. "Kit! I didn't know you were a Teamster."

Kit Kline turned his back on me, leaning against the bar. "For now."

The last time we'd met had been at the Avalon Ballroom, where, in spite of our many political differences, Kit had gotten a hard-on dancing with me. His attitude toward me had obviously changed.

I stepped up beside him. The bar was a tiny, makeshift affair, littered with cocktail napkins and empty plastic cups, which a yawning bartender made no effort to clear away. "What local are you with?"

"Sixteen."

The Avalon Ballroom had closed more than ten years ago, but Kit didn't look much older. He was a little heavier, but as pale as ever, with the same chronically dissatisfied mouth and scowling brow. He'd been a Trotskyite for a while, a pain in the ass at every political meeting he'd attended, seizing the floor and shouting the same tired polemics. Then it had been cocaine and, as I recalled, a Ph.D. in the history of consciousness from U.C. Santa Cruz.

"Are you a business agent?" Business agents organize workers, negotiate contracts, and file unfair labor practice charges with the National Labor Relations Board. The job requires delicacy and tact, but rarely attracts anyone with those qualities.

"For Local 16," Kline repeated dourly. "Semi had the fucking balls to tell me he'd kick my butt out of here if I showed up this weekend."

I scanned the room, looking for Semi Sawyer. As secretary-treasurer of Kline's local, Semi had the undisputed right to kick Kline's butt—a right I was beginning to envy. "I gather you're a Teamsters for a Democratic Union man."

"Fucking right."

"I'm sorry about Jim Zissner."

"Yeah, I'll fucking bet you are."

"Why shouldn't I be?"

"You guys are all in bed with Semi." He waved his hand dismissively. "Tell you this much: if Zissner'd won the election we'd have dropped Kerrey like a hot rock. How the fuck did you end up working for Mr. Nicey-nice Liberal, anyway?"

"Warneke, Kerrey's the leftiest of all the lefty law firms," I pointed out, knowing that, to some radicals, it's worse to be merely liberal than it is to be far right. "Didn't Julian Warneke represent you once on a possession charge?"

"Yeah. And I got six months. For a lousy gram of hash."

Mr. Nicey-nice Liberal himself joined us. Clement greeted Kit, expressing his sympathy about Zissner.

Kit nodded without looking at him. After a polite pause,

Clement turned to me. "Willa, I want to introduce you to Claire and Marge from Local 154."

He pulled me over to two overly made-up business agents wearing half a ton of jewelry between them. We talked about gambling and the naked statues in the lobby.

By the time I escaped them, Kit was nowhere to be seen. Nor did he reappear when we were finally seated for dinner.

By doing some quick scrambling, I was able to sit beside Semi Sawyer, who was too drunk to care that I was his lawyer, and just drunk enough to want to sit beside a "young gal" like me. From his behavior I deduced that he had no general objection to Teamsters sleeping with their lawyers; his objection to Mae and Jim's affair had been politics, not principle.

By dessert, Semi's thick black hair, long on top and combed straight back, was falling over his forehead, and he was finding too many excuses to touch me. I said, "Too bad about Jim Zissner."

That got his hand off my knee. He took a swallow of whiskey and didn't respond.

"I hear some troublemaker in Retail Clerks is trying to implicate—"

"Bunch of crap." There was no heat in his tone. "Don't take a tractor on a stretch of road like that. Guy's full of bullshit—pardon my French."

"Is TDU going to run someone else in Zissner's place?"

Semi looked around the room, as if suddenly bored with me. "I imagine."

"Do you know who?"

"Maybe Kline." He took a cigar offered to him by a passerby. With a curt, "Nice talking to you," he pushed back his chair and went off to slap some backs.

Clement slipped into the chair Semi had vacated, smiling his broadest smile. "Isn't he a hell of a guy?"

"A saint," I agreed.

The light went out of Clement's eyes for a moment, but I smiled, forcing him to smile back.

"We've got a meeting in the morning with some folks from Local 92. Conference room three at ten o'clock, all right?"

I was thus formally excused. I went up to my room, got stoned, and watched the movie channel until I passed out.

• CHAPTER TWENTY •

The conference room had a mirrored ceiling. Every time I glanced up, I saw myself upside down and backward, which is pretty much how I felt that morning anyway.

Sitting with me were three Teamsters: the secretary-treasurer of Local 92, who introduced himself as "Just Hank! Don't 'mister' me!"; a thirtyish woman with a thin ponytail and K-Mart clothes; and her fellow business agent, a finger-tapping, foot-twitching bundle of impatient mannerisms.

We were waiting for Clement Kerrey. And since I didn't know a thing about Local 92's problems, conversation was strained. By the time Clement was twenty minutes late, the business agent's tattooing, grunting, and watch checking had driven me out of my chair. I braved the Boschian lobby and asked the desk clerk for Clement's room number. Then I went upstairs to find room 223.

As I got off the elevator, I saw Clement closing the door to room 214. He dashed down the hall and around a corner.

I followed in less haste and found him punching the down button of another bank of elevators. He glanced at me, hitting the button again. "Local 92. I'm late. I know." He was flushed and out of breath. He didn't speak to me in the elevator. He stood straight and motionless, clutching his briefcase, his black eyes gleaming under his straight gray brows. I was reminded of something Felix had said about Clement, that sometimes you could almost hear his disk drives whirring.

I had to run to keep up with him as we crossed the

lobbyful of gamblers. I bumped into a white-haired lady who had a drink and cigarette in one hand and a slot handle in the other. "*I'm* playing this machine!" she muttered crossly. From a raised central island, a man with a game-show voice called out the names and hometowns of jackpot winners, and mini-togaed women with chilled white flesh ran keno cards. Clement pushed through them, obliviously.

When we got to the conference room, Clement apologized with his usual show of sincerity and pulled a sheaf of papers from his briefcase.

Hank Don't-mister-me emitted a sound somewhere between a chuckle and a groan.

Clement nodded sourly. "That's right. Declarations—statements by witnesses saying you—"

"Aw, hell, Clement! We didn't do anything!" Hank's lips smiled, but his grizzled brows were pinched. "It's all a buncha bull tweet!"

The ponytailed woman glanced at her fellow business agent, her eyes narrowed. I couldn't tell whether she was amused or angry. A face like hers belonged at the blackjack table.

"Well," Clement continued calmly, "we can hardly ignore these, people. There are some pretty serious charges here."

"Bull tweet!" Hank repeated, dabbing his forehead with a polyester sleeve. "You know how it goes during a strike. Sure, the boys get mad—they got every reason to get mad. Company's run by a bunch of goddam criminals! But we didn't do anything. Just blew off a little steam."

Clement scanned the topmost Declaration. "I hear what you're saying, Hank, I really do. But the company manager, Brad Hickley, says two of your men pulled him out of a truck and beat him—"

"Hickley's a goddam liar! It's a goddam lie! He's out to bust the union!" Hank's cheeks grew redder as he waved his arm. "Hell, I know those two guys—they wouldn't hurt a fly! They wouldn't—"

"According to this," Clement cut in wryly, "Stevens admitted—"

"Well, goddam it!" Hank shouted. "Hickley had it coming! Him and Wilson were running in scabs in company trailers—picking 'em up down in Salinas like cattle and blasting through the picket line— If I hadn't pulled her out of the way, they'da run Mary Gomez down, for Christsake!"

"All right, all right," Clement soothed. "Let's put this one aside for a minute. What about this star nail business? I've got three Declarations here saying that on April twentieth Tom Gelbar and Rudy Cipola threw star nails all over the road behind the company's back gate."

"No way!" Hank shook his head emphatically. "Not Gelbar and Cipola! They weren't even around then!"

"I saw Cipola bending the nails out behind the loading dock," the poker-faced woman replied.

"Hell, Cipola didn't even join the union till May!"

"He joined in March," she contradicted.

"Well, okay, okay, maybe he was a member. But Jesus H. McGillicuddy! A handful of star nails! What's the big deal?"

Clement sighed, frowning down at the Declarations. "It says here the company gathered over two hundred nails off the road—"

"They don't hardly do any damage, anyway!"

"—after the nails had ruined the tires of three rigs!"

The impatient young man sat up straighter in his chair. "Does it say there what Hickley's fucking scabs did? We got two men in the hospital right now! Mary Gomez is still black and blue where Hickley's truck hit her! Fucker called the cops on us on Good Friday—ruined everyone's Easter, right?—and hell, we were two hundred fucking yards away from the gate! Jesus, I've seen Hickley—"

"We'll be talking about that in a little bit!" Clement

reassured him, flipping through the Declarations. "Right now let's see if we can straighten out which of our people did what, and what it's going to mean in terms of our contract negotiations."

"Two guys in the hospital—and you don't want to talk about it?" The young man stood up, glowering across the table.

Clement continued shuffling through the Declarations.

Hank reached out and grabbed the young man's arm, trying to jerk him back into his seat. "We don't want to eat any more shit than we have to, Clement! What are we talking about here?"

"The company's prepared to file criminal charges, Hank. That's no big deal in itself, but it almost guarantees they'll get their restraining order."

Hank turned "shit" into a four-syllable word.

"I can try to limit it to numbers and spacing again, but"—Clement shrugged—"you've already violated one numbers and spacing order."

"Hell, Adolf H. Hitler could have written that order!"

"The best thing," Clement continued calmly, "would be to get them to drop the whole thing and come back to the bargaining table. Which they might do, if we let them use these"—he tapped the stack of Declarations—"as a bargaining chip."

The young man, still on his feet, erupted, "Bargaining chip! Hell, Hickley doesn't want to bargain! He wants to bust this mother-loving union!"

Hank behaved as if the young man hadn't spoken. "So how about deferring company payments into the pension fund for a few months?"

Clement nodded slowly. "That might work. Reinstatement for all striking workers at full previous salary and benefits—"

"*Previous* salary?" The young man was growing purple

with outrage. "Part of the reason we went out on the line was their piss-poor cost-of-living adjustment!"

"Without the hours reductions they proposed, naturally!" Clement's gaze remained calmly on Hank. "And in exchange for their stipulation not to file charges or seek restitution for property damage, they defer payment into the pension fund until November, say. Saving them," he squinted thoughtfully, "forty-five thousand dollars, plus or minus."

"Hell," Hank nodded, "they're not gonna go after an order if it costs 'em forty-five grand to get it!"

The young man pounded the table. "You're gonna let this shyster sell out the union for a measly forty-five—!"

"Pardon me, pardon me!" A pale man in a Caesar's blazer had entered the room. "Mr. Kerrey?" He looked around the table, his face twitching with agitation.

Clement did not seem surprised to see the man. Without inquiring why he was wanted, he gathered up his papers and followed the blazered man out into the hall.

The young man glared at Hank for a moment and then shouted, "Screw this shit, Hank! Screw you!" And he stomped out, too.

Hank and the ponytailed woman exchanged long-suffering glances. Hank smiled ruefully. "He's a good organizer, but he's not much of a compromiser."

"Teamsters for a Democratic Union?" I surmised.

Again Hank and the woman exchanged glances. "So happens," Hank confirmed. "He's not as bad as he used to be, now he's been a business agent for a while. But he still doesn't understand about restraining orders. Hell, if you gotta move your picketers to the other side of kingdom come, what's the point? You get guys crossing the line, not even knowing there is one. You might as well call off the strike and go back to bed."

Clement poked his head back inside. "I'm sorry, Hank. Something's come up. An emergency."

He didn't stick around to tell us what.

When I walked the Local 92 people out to the lobby, I noticed uniformed cops beside the reservation desk, huddling with men in hotel blazers. Clement Kerrey, his back to us, was standing with them, shaking his head to questions I couldn't hear.

I said good-bye to Hank Don't-mister-me and joined Clement. His head was bowed, and he didn't turn toward me. A policeman was saying something about jurisdiction and about calling San Francisco as a courtesy. I thought at first that Clement didn't notice me standing there. But when a hotel manager requested that "she" be moved as soon as possible, Clement put his arm around me.

Sotto voce, he murmured, "They found Mae Siegel upstairs. Willa, she's dead."

• CHAPTER TWENTY-ONE •

The joint council continued for two more days, but the only other function I attended was a banquet the final night.

I didn't want to go to *it*, either. I made that clear to Clement.

"Why don't we dance on Mae's grave while we're at it?" I could feel my fingers snaking into my hair; and I'd almost broken myself of the habit, damn it.

"I hear what you're saying, Willa." Clement lounged on a dirty velveteen chair in my room, waiting for me to slip on my jacket and accompany him downstairs. A lace bra dangled over the chair arm beneath his hand, but he didn't seem to notice. "And you know I loved Mae, too. But our clients need to know we're there for them, no matter what."

I'd known Clement Kerrey most of my life, and like everyone else, I'd always thought of him as Mr. Decent. But Mae Siegel had died in room 214, and I'd begun to wonder whether Conversational Nice Guy was just a foreign language Clement had mastered.

But I was determined not to say, as movie heroines are wont to do, "I saw you coming out of Mae Siegel's room the morning she was murdered." I was that worried about Clement Kerrey.

Nor had I informed the police. They had fancy fingerprint techniques, fiber analyses, coroners, pathologists, and other experts. They didn't need information from me, and I didn't need grief from a possibly murderous boss.

I slipped on my black wool jacket and went to the banquet.

• CHAPTER TWENTY-TWO •

Semi Sawyer looked at my suit and smirked, "Don't you lady lawyers ever wear dresses?"

He was wearing the Teamster version of black tie—a dark suit, light yellow shirt, and string tie with a tiger's-eye clasp.

I'd just downed a whiskey-and-seven on an empty stomach. "Did you hear what happened to Mae Siegel?"

Semi's fleshy face grew stonily expressionless: a contract negotiator's face. "Heard she found Mr. Goodbar."

Mae Siegel had been suffocated in her bed, probably with a motel pillow. I should have guessed people would assume—

"We're very upset about Mae." Clement Kerrey materialized at my side. "She'd been with us a long time." He put his arm around me tightly, warningly.

I wriggled out of Clement's grasp. The bastard would have fired Mae just because a bellicose Teamster didn't like her sleeping with his political opponent.

Both men made me sick.

I pushed through clusters of laughing, gossiping Teamsters and got myself another whiskey-and-seven. I spotted Kit Kline slumped alone at a corner table, nursing a tall, sweating drink.

I sat beside him. He didn't look at me.

I drank a little more whiskey (give me pot any day). "What's with the James Dean impersonation?"

Kit waved his left arm. Close by, Hank Don't-mister-me of Local 92 was praising the recently indicted president of

Teamsters International. "These morons would defend Josef Mengele if he were president! 'Friend of the working man,' my ass!"

"Come on, Kit! It's pro forma for every new administration to harass the Teamsters. They're a safe target, like government waste or drug—"

"Blind loyalty! That's what it is! What's it matter if the union's full of crooks!"

"Crooks! Look around. These people worked in canneries, drove trucks, delivered pizzas, sewed clothes. Maybe the International's done a couple of shady things, but you've got no complaint with the people here. Don't tell me you think they're—"

"You're so fucking naive!"

"And you're a fool!" I gulped what was left of my drink. "Same damn thing as the peace movement—try to organize against the war, and you Trotskyites disrupt everything—no ideas of your own—too busy criticizing and blathering about a general strike—as if people—hell, we couldn't even get McGovern elected and you guys wanted—we were stupid to even let you take the floor—" Listening to myself ramble about politics, circa 1972, it occurred to me that I was drunk.

"Oh, yeah? Take the fucking floor?" Kit's voice wavered on a high note. Heads turned. "You fucking pulled the plug on our mikes at the People's Peace Treaty Conference, remember that?"

I smiled at the memory. How sweet it is to silence an ideologue.

Kit leaped to his feet, bumping his chair into the table behind him. "Fucking Teamster leadership, fucking Sleazy Sawyer's not pulling my plug this time. No way!"

Around us, conversations ceased.

And from his jacket pocket, Kit Kline produced a chrome-colored gun.

I could feel the whiskey burning a hole in my stomach.

The room began to rock. I tried to think of something to say. I came up with, "Jeez."

There was a sudden flash of movement beside me, and a moment later Kit Kline was supine on the table. His gun clattered to the floor. Holding him down was Local 92's business agent, the Teamsters for a Democratic Union man who'd stormed out of the mirrored-ceiling conference room two mornings before.

I was probably the only person in the room close enough to hear what he murmured to Kit Kline. It was hardly more than a rumble in the business agent's throat, but there was no hint of sarcasm in the tone. Before several strong Teamsters fell on them and shuffled Kit out of the room, I heard the business agent whisper to Kit, "Nice work!"

Nice work! What the hell did that mean?

I became the center of a curious group. I told them Kit had been showing me his gun, which a Teamster now retrieved from under the table. I told them Kit's movements had been abrupt because he'd been drunk. The Teamsters looked at one another. They didn't believe me. Hank Don't-mister-me patted my shoulder. "We liked what you said about the union. That punk gives you any more trouble, you call me!" He took the gun from his fellow Teamster, and sauntered out of the room with it.

After a while, Clement Kerrey joined us. He said Kit Kline (and his gun) had been turned over to hotel security but that there was no talk of filing criminal charges. "I understand he was a close friend of Jim Zissner's and that this has been an upsetting time for him." Clement looked around the group, inviting others to share his compassion.

The woman with half a ton of jewelry (Marge? Claire?) took his arm and pressed her breasts against him. "You're a prince, Clement!"

The saintliness of Clement's smile put my parents' icons to shame.

Nice work. What object had Kline achieved, that a fellow TDU man would call it "nice work"? If anything, Kit had cast in iron the stereotype of the TDU hothead. If anything, he'd guaranteed Semi Sawyer's reelection.

I looked around. Semi stood at the bar puffing his cigar, the slightest hint of a smile on his broad face.

The next day, on the long car ride home to San Francisco, I asked Clement how serious a threat Zissner had posed to Semi.

"You know how it is. Semi's been secretary-treasurer, what, fourteen years now. It's easy for the flakier members to blame things on him, everything from canneries shutting down to dues increases. Truth is, these are hard times for unions. We've got an unsympathetic Labor Board, and," he shrugged, "people are more reactionary. They don't like unions, and even if they did, they'd be afraid to organize because the boss might get mad and move the operation down to Puerto Rico. Not much Semi can do about that, but he catches the flak."

"So Zissner might have won the election?"

Clement nodded. "Might have. Zissner was a clever guy. A populist—liked to call himself the thinking man's working man. He appealed to the younger members."

"Is there anyone else like that in Local 16? Anyone else who could beat Semi?"

Clement's brows pinched as he watched the road. "Until last night I'd have said Kline had an outside chance. You know, indirect sympathy vote for Zissner."

"Kline told me Zissner would have switched law firms if he'd won the election."

Clement was silent for the next mile or two.

"I've heard Semi complain about our retainer fee, Clement. Is that part of the problem?"

"That's just Semi. As much work as we do for the local, he knows our retainer's artificially low. It's like I told him this morning: we love the work for its own sake and for the union's sake, but we're a business, too." He glanced at me. "Teamster retainers have been frozen since nineteen seventy-five. And with all the work we do for them," he shook his head, "we end up losing money on the account. Julian—he was a wonderful man, the very best—but he was sending us right into Chapter Eleven. I can't remember the last time we turned enough of a profit to pull partnership shares. And then he goes and hires a new—" Clement patted my knee. "Not that you haven't done a great job for us."

I wondered if his statement presaged a pink slip.

• CHAPTER TWENTY-THREE •

On the table in my bay window were some more hate letters. Funny how worked up strangers can get about things that don't concern them and about which they know nothing (as witness the letters-to-the-editor page of any newspaper). The letter that interested me most contained details about the law school I'd attended; its accusations had clearly come from a fellow alumnus. There are some crazy lawyers out there. Not that I needed the letter as proof.

Still, anonymous hatred, especially in a city full of lunatics, tends to make a person feel vulnerable. So I was glad to see Don Surgelato, for once. I opened my apartment door to him and even catered to his instinctive nosiness by showing him the letter from my fellow Malhousie alumn.

He shrugged it off; I guess it takes at least a mutilated corpse to perturb a homicide lieutenant. "You heard about the sentence?"

I pointed to my evening paper. The headline read, LAW SCHOOL MURDERER SENTENCED. "Fifteen years."

"Know what that works out to, per person? *Assuming* the killer serves maybe two-thirds of the term—which, hell, with good behavior, we'd be lucky— Or what the trial cost the city? One-point-two million!"

I had no reason to be angry with the lieutenant, except that he reminded me of things I wanted to forget. "Is that why you're not catching *this* killer? It's thriftier not to?"

Surgelato looked peaked, as skinny as his barrel-chested,

Italianate frame would allow. His skin looked pasty and his coarse hair had thinned on top, making his brows seem even thicker, even lower. "Look, I'm trying to keep this friendly, but you know something?" He dropped into a director's chair. "You're the only goddam person who was at all three murder scenes. You were sitting with Warneke when he got it, you were at your office when Mrs. Warneke—"

"She was alive when I left."

"By way of the fire escape! And you were at Caesar's when—" He stopped, squinting at me. "You knew Mae Siegel was there? Was she supposed to be there?"

"No to both questions."

"So what was she doing?"

"I don't know. Except that— Do you understand Teamster politics?" I explained about Jim Zissner and the Teamsters for a Democratic Union, about the upcoming election, and Zissner's chances of winning it. "Mae was Zissner's girlfriend. So she was particularly *non grata* with some of the people at the council."

Surgelato pulled out a notebook and pen with University of San Francisco logos. I spelled out some names for him. Local 16 wouldn't appreciate it, but I needed a favor from the lieutenant. I added, "René's, the restaurant where Julian— where we had lunch that day. It's Teamster, too. Did you know that? Local 16."

Surgelato put his notebook away, watching me.

"I don't usually volunteer information, I know. But I appreciate the fact that you're keeping things friendly."

"Do you, now?"

"And I thought as long as you were feeling friendly, you might answer a question for me."

"Depends on the question, of course. If it doesn't involve this case—"

"It does. But if I knew the answer— Look, if I fill you in

on some office gossip—" I hesitated; I didn't want to implicate Clement. It seemed subversive.

"Miss Jansson," his tone verged on exasperation. "It's your civic and professional duty to cooperate with us in this investigation. We don't trade information."

I sat opposite him, so close our knees almost touched. "Look, I'll be honest with you, Lieutenant. Julian wasn't my mentor or anything. I didn't even think he was a particularly good lawyer." My fingers found their way into my hair, but I was past caring. "He probably got as many people into trouble as out of it—to him trials were theater. My trial was. My defense—I didn't realize until I went to law school how lame it was—Julian called it self-defense against governmental terrorism. I mean, my parents are willing to go to jail to make a political statement, but me— I spent two months sewing curtains! Blue lace curtains! That's what the matron made us do. I have no idea why. It still makes me vomit to look at a sewing machine!"

I stood up; what the hell was I doing, anyway? "I spent two months of my life living for one hour a week—Saturday from three to four, visiting hour. But see, at the time, the way Julian presented it to me, and with my parents the way they are— But then when I started working for Julian, I don't know, I saw that he wasn't a firebrand, you know, like the Trotskyites were, or the Weathermen. He wasn't doing it because he had to, emotionally, to live with himself. It was more cerebral than that. The day he died he was sitting there telling me to turn my trial—I'm preparing a jury trial for a kid who didn't register with the selective service—Julian wanted me to turn it into a big political show. And I thought, shit, here's Julian eating a fifty-dollar lunch and telling me to blow this kid's trial just so I can get up on a fucking soapbox!"

I could feel tears spring to my eyes. Surgelato seemed surprised. I was, too. "I started out to tell you how much I liked Julian and how much I want you to find out who killed him. And I do. I did like him. I didn't admire him, but— I've known him for years. Jesus! And I want to know why—" I bit my lip; I was at the border of Too Far.

"Why he bequeathed his house to your mother?"

"Just tell me one thing. Answer one question."

"You said you had some office gossip for me."

"And then you'll answer—"

"It depends on the question. I'll tell you what I can; that's all I can promise. But I want the gossip first."

I sat back down, glancing at my tableful of hate mail. My neck ached. "Julian might have been about to dissolve his partnership with Clement Kerrey. That's what Matthilde Warneke says. That Julian was going to dissolve the partnership and leave Clement with just the labor clients."

There was very little daylight left; Surgelato's face was a gray wash with deep shadows at the eyes and in the cleft of his Dudley Do-Right chin. I continued. "I asked Clement about those clients. He says Julian froze their retainer fees at nineteen seventy-five levels, and that the firm does so much work for them, it actually loses money. Especially on Local 16. Clement's always in court for them. He said Julian was ruining the business, and that the partners haven't been making money—"

"Warneke pulled in fifty-six thousand, five, salary."

"As the senior partner of a fifteen-year-old firm. Starting salary on Wall Street is sixty-five thousand—and that's for a kid fresh out of law school. Julian could have earned three, four times that in another kind of practice. And to hear Clement tell it, he could have earned a lot more in his own practice."

"Yeah, well, you want a good laugh sometime, I'll tell you how much I make."

"Did Edward Hershey tell you why Bess Warneke phoned him from Julian's office?"

Surgelato's brows rose. "I can't discuss that."

"Did he tell you she knew something that would invalidate Julian's will?"

He sat forward, his elbow on his knee, rubbing his chin. "I can't—"

"That's what Hershey told me. That Bess said she might have some proof. And all I want to know is, did you find it? Did you find anything in Julian's office that—"

"Why?"

"Why what?"

"Why do you want to know?"

"Because I want to believe there are external causes for all these murders. Problems that preceded my joining the firm." I brushed the letters off the table. "This is bad enough: nut cases hating me for no good reason! And having to keep my phone off the hook all the time because of reporters. And Hershey—that's a long story. Look, all I want is a little information. To prove it's not *me*, that I'm not some kind of Homicide Mary."

Surgelato stood up, sighing. I could see the outline of a holstered gun on his hip. "Every case, we get somebody wants to be Sherlock Holmes. We'll do our best, but you gotta leave it to us. You know what I mean?"

I stepped closer to him. "Help me out, Lieutenant. I think about it all the time, but I don't have enough information to know what makes sense and what doesn't."

He put a thick-fingered hand on my neck, as if to massage the tensed muscle. "Look, I'll tell you this much—but it's my ass if you do anything stupid with the information."

"I won't."

"Wasn't a damned thing in Warneke's office, not a thing in his bank accounts, his papers, anything, to back up what Hershey told us. Maybe we just haven't found it yet; or maybe Mrs. Warneke was bitter and just wanted to believe there was something; or maybe whoever killed her took the information out of Warneke's office." Surgelato squinted. "Or it could be Hershey's lying."

His hand was still on my neck. His fingers were very warm, almost hot. Bess lying or Hershey lying; where did that information get me?

Surgelato stepped away stiffly, looking uncomfortable, even a little angry. "I'll check on this partnership deal of Kerrey's. Thanks."

Watching him, recalling the things I'd blurted out, especially about the curtains, about visiting day, I became intensely uncomfortable myself. I bent down and began scooping up my letters.

When Surgelato spoke again, it was from the doorway. "I'll be in touch," he said curtly. Then he stomped out, slamming the door. I heard him hesitate on the landing before he ran down the stairs.

• CHAPTER TWENTY-FOUR •

Felix Flish popped his head into Julian's office. "Here before eight again?" He was in rolled-up shirt-sleeves and stockinged feet. He looked around the denuded office. "Spooky place."

"Did the police take the photographs?" The peasant sketches were still on Julian's walls, but the framed snapshots were gone.

Felix shrugged. "Might have been Matthilde."

"Are you two having an affair?"

His eyes widened. "You flatter me."

"You're flattered? That I accuse you of sleeping with your mentor's wife?"

"Mentor? Whoa! I wouldn't describe Julian as my—"

"Matthilde says you spent a lot of time at their house. She says Julian told her he'd 'guaranteed' your future."

"Why would Julian do that for his wife's lover?"

"Why would he make you a partner after only two years?"

"You want to know why he made me a partner? Truly? No joke?"

I nodded, expecting a lie, expecting a joke.

"Clement's practice is practically pro bono. Brian spends all his time on 'client development'—which is a polite way of saying he buys a lot of people lunch—and Julian, well, Julian had already made a name for himself, and he wasn't going to ruin his reputation by trying any more cases." Felix grinned.

"And meanwhile, my pretty, who do you suppose has been paying this firm's bills?" He clapped his hand to his chest.

"But isn't that traditional? Associates do all the work and partners—"

"It may be traditional, but I didn't go to Stanford Law School to be an underpaid wage slave. One or the other, maybe, but not both."

"So you decided to become one of the bosses?"

"You red-diaper babies! You really know the jargon." He did the collie routine with his eyebrows. "Yes, I decided to become one of the bosses. I gave Julian an ultimatum. If I was going to carry the firm on my back, I wanted my name on the door. Or I'd go someplace where the pay was commensurate with the workload."

"And Julian went for it?"

"It was either that or do the work himself. Besides," Felix observed, "it's not like being a partner in this firm gets you any more money."

"So why did you want it?"

He leaned against the bare wall. "I think I can turn the firm around. Financially, I mean, not philosophically."

"By getting rid of Clement?"

His fingers traced the outline of an unfaded square where a picture had lately hung. "Why do you say that?"

"Because the labor practice loses money. You just said so. Even Clement admits it."

"It doesn't generate enough income to pay Clement's salary and overhead," he mused, "but there's a lot of goodwill associated with being one of the best labor firms in the state. It brings in other kinds of clients. Beside, Clement's starting to negotiate more realistic retainers."

"Why didn't he do it sooner? Why did he wait until Julian died?"

"You've seen our letterhead, cookie. Warneke, Kerrey, Lieberman & Flish, A Legal Corporation. We call ourselves partners, but technically we're shareholders. And the unfortunate fact was, Julian owned three shares and we each owned one."

"What about Brian?"

"What about him?"

"Does he make money for the firm?"

Felix seemed to measure my height and gauge my weight. "Brian's the laziest lawyer I've ever met. But in all fairness, he does bring in accounts. And his political connections are useful. He can get on the horn and ask his buddy the legislator to block a lousy bill—lousy for the firm, I mean. Like AB 342. It would have taxed our— Anyway, the point is, you can't really quantify that."

"So it was Julian."

"What was Julian?"

"The deadwood. Julian was the deadwood in this law firm."

Felix pushed himself off the wall. "An unfortunate metaphor."

I went back to my office and made some phone calls. The first was to Matthilde Warneke. "That paper you showed me, dissolving the partnership—are you sure it was Julian's idea?"

"What do you mean?"

"Did he ever mention it to you?"

"No. I—" There was a hint of confusion in her voice. "I found it. Bill Ingram said you went to see him."

"Yes. Do you know if Felix suggested it to Julian? Dissolving the partnership?"

"I found the paper," she repeated sharply. "I already told you. That's *all* I know about it."

"I don't remember the phrasing, Matthilde. Did it leave Brian and Felix free to join Clement?"

"Why would they want to do that?"

"No reason, but did it?"

"It offered Clement 'the fair market value of his share, to

be determined by an independent auditor'—something like that. It didn't say anything about Felix or Brian."

I shook my head; the information wasn't integrating itself into an insight. I guess I wasn't up to psychosynthesizing so early in the morning. "You said Bess took all Julian's antiques, things the court had awarded to Julian. How did she do it?"

"She emptied the house when we were in Europe."

"On your honeymoon?"

"Our tour, yes. You can imagine how we felt when we got back. Julian had already given her too much!"

"He kept the house."

Anger strained her voice. "Julian was entitled to *something* after working his whole life!"

"So what did Bess get? What was there, besides the house and furniture?"

"Oh, bank accounts, you know. Insurance policies. Is this important?"

"No other land, no other real estate?"

"I told you. Bank accounts."

"The value of real estate's shot way up these last few years. But money's different, it hasn't—"

"So what? What are you saying?"

"Nothing. Thanks."

My second call was to Santa Cruz. Edward Hershey answered his own phone; too broke to afford a secretary, I hoped.

"You lied to me."

"Actually, honey, you lied to me."

"Don't call me honey! You said Bess had proof something was wrong with Julian's will. Well, the cops didn't find anything. They didn't find any evidence Julian's will was—"

"The cops told you that?"

"You lied. If Bess phoned you at all, she didn't phone you about the will!"

"They actually told you they didn't find anything?" His

breathing grew audible. "So maybe it wasn't a *thing*. Maybe it was a *what*."

We breathed at one another for a moment. Then he said, more quietly, "Tell me something; I'm curious. Hasn't there ever been a single time, just one time, when you sincerely believed the virus was dormant—no, no, listen to me—when you sincerely believed it was safe to skip the warning?"

I felt adrenaline flood my system; it was like being dunked in ice water. "No! I've never skipped the warning."

"Well! Not that you'll give a darn, but I haven't since."

I slammed down the receiver and pushed the phone away. I stood up and paced. Goddam him—safe to skip the warning!

I looked out my window at the blank facade of the parking garage across the street. Sure, I'd wanted to believe it was safe, often enough. And I'd come damn close, a time or two.

I went back to the phone and made my third call. "Manuel. Hi. I tried to return your call last week."

There was a pause before Manuel Boyd said, "Hello." The word was spoken tentatively.

"My landlord said he talked to you the other day."

"Uh-huh." It was a moment before he spoke again; I was used to Manuel's silent stutter. "He's an interesting man."

"He said you asked him about Martin Rittenhaus."

His pause was longer than usual; something was up. "You've seen *The Night of March Nineteenth*?"

"Several times."

"I saw it after Warneke died. You know, background. I interviewed some of the people in it. They gave me names of other people who knew Warneke back then."

"You did this for the *Chronicle*? They don't usually print more than four paragraphs on any topic other than—"

"Dieting, I know. But—"

The pause was so long, I had to ask, "What?"

"I met a woman— You should talk to her. I'd be interested to hear what you think of her story."

"Who is she?"

"She was Warneke and Rittenhaus's paralegal. I could set up an appointment for us to see her. Would you want to?"

"What's it about?"

"You should hear it from her. You might not get the same thing out of it that I got. I mean, you knew Warneke, and I didn't."

"I'm going to federal court this afternoon to watch a judge voir dire my jury."

"I'll bring her to your office? This morning?" Manuel's statements usually sounded like questions.

"All right."

I hung up and reviewed my proposed voir dire questions. Judge Rondi had denied every one of my pretrial motions; he would probably ignore my proposed questions, too. I'd probably end up with a jury as fascistic as my judge.

I resorted to a childhood comfort. I placed a finger on my third eye, and a finger on each nostril. I breathed in through my right nostril, counting to eight. Held my breath for a count of sixteen; breathed out through my left nostril, counting to eight; held without breath, one, two, three, four; breathed in through the left; held for sixteen . . .

After a few minutes, I was forced to admit that my *sati* was beyond repair.

• CHAPTER TWENTY-FIVE •

Manuel Boyd stood with his hips thrust forward and his arms folded into the hollow of his belly. His bone-thin, sharp-featured face drooped toward his chest, but he watched me attentively. He'd lost a great deal of hair, and his olive complexion looked yellow-gray. When I'd met him two years earlier, he'd been heavier, his posture had been better, and he'd looked ten years younger. I supposed reporting for a major newspaper was harder work than freelancing for an artsy tabloid.

The woman standing beside him looked to be fifteen or twenty years his senior; and yet, she gave the impression of greater vigor. She was short, even shorter than me, with chopped brown curls, a lot of laugh wrinkles and freckles, and sparkling black eyes that swiftly took in every detail of my office. She seated herself in the molded vinyl chair, tucking her hands into her overall pockets and kicking the more comfortable, padded chair toward Manuel.

"I think I know your mother," was the first thing the woman said to me. "What a dear!"

"She is that." I looked to Manuel for an introduction.

He sat on his lower spine, his long legs extended in front of him. "Gayle Halberstam," he obliged me.

She smiled at him; something about the smile, something that shouldn't have been there, disturbed me. Apparently it disturbed Manuel, too; he frowned slightly.

"I used to work for Julian and Martin," Gayle Halberstam volunteered. "I worked my fanny off; I've never worked so hard in my life, but I loved it!" She drew out the "o" in "loved"; I was conscious of disliking it, and worried that I was becoming a crank.

Gayle slid to the edge of her chair. "I didn't tell anybody about this. I still wouldn't go to the pigs with it!"

I thought of Surgelato; there was a lot wrong with him, but I didn't like hearing him called a pig. (By god, I *was* turning into a crank!)

"But . . ." She looked at Manuel. He nodded. "I guess I can trust you not to go to the cops. Your mama brought you up better than that!"

I didn't contradict her.

"March nineteenth," she continued, "the day— I guess everybody knows that date! That morning—it was a Friday; Martin and Julian used to do their time sheets on Friday so Sally could do the billing on Monday—Sally had a question about Martin's timesheet and she went in to ask him about it. She tapped at the door like she always did; then she opened it. God, I can just see her in her jeans! We used to wear jeans to work—isn't that great! That was Julian's doing—Martin would have had us in suits, but Julian—! Anyway, Sally opened the door, and I was walking by on my way to the copy machine. I heard her ask where Martin was, which I thought was strange, since it was his office." She frowned, not at me, but at some memory.

"This was six or seven hours before Rittenhaus went to Folsom prison to visit Harlen Pryce?" I wondered why I should care who'd been in Rittenhaus's office that morning—or what his secretaries had been wearing.

"Do you remember the warden's press conference, after the shoot-out?" Gayle Halberstam was still frowning. "Where he explained how Martin was supposed to have smuggled the gun in to Harlen?"

I nodded. "In a tape recorder in his briefcase."

"Not that I believe it—the prison probably lied about the whole thing, beginning to end."

That was the conclusion Bill Ingram had drawn in his documentary: that two guards had shot down the charismatic Pryce in cold blood, to keep him from revealing systematic prisoner abuse; that one of them had tossed a gun beside Pryce's dead body to justify the murder; and that the warden had been willing, even happy, to offer up Martin Rittenhaus as a scapegoat. Rittenhaus had been a thorn in the warden's side for years, inundating him in temporary restraining orders restricting his ability to isolate "violent" prisoners, forcing him to open a law library for prisoners, forcing him to honor the (expensive) dietary restrictions of Black Muslims.

"For one thing," Gayle Halberstam continued, "Martin never used a tape recorder; our clients didn't like it. You remember that era—nobody would let themselves be tape-recorded or fingerprinted or photographed. And Martin didn't dictate letters, he used to type up drafts himself—Sally just loved him for it." Again, the cheerfully long "o." "But I was thinking—and I don't mean to sound disloyal or be making too much out of this—but Julian had a tape recorder. He used to dictate into it, and Sally would put on headphones and type his stuff up."

I glanced at my own tiny tape recorder; almost everyone dictated these days.

She followed my glance. "Oh, gosh, they were nowhere near that small back then." She held up her hands, defining a rectangle about nine by seven. "They were like so. Julian's was, anyway. It had a hard case."

"You think Martin took Julian's tape recorder out of its case and put a gun inside?" Among people of our political persuasion, to admit such a possibility was heresy.

"Oh, no. No. What I'm thinking is worse, maybe, in a way. I don't know. I mean, this is just something I thought of; I loved Julian—really. But when Sally opened Martin's door and asked where Martin was, I peeked in and saw Julian closing Martin's briefcase. Martin used to leave it on his chair whenever he went out without it.''

I glanced at Manuel. He was hugging himself, his cheeks sucked into hollow sockets. Why had he brought me this woman, with her inconsequential memories?

"You're not suggesting Julian put a gun into Martin's—?"

Felix Flish opened my door, his long, lean torso swinging into view, one hand on the door frame to keep him from falling forward. "Willa, did I tell you—? Oops! Sorry, folks!" He glanced curiously at Gayle Halberstam and Manuel Boyd, then wadded up a pink telephone message slip and tossed it onto my desk.

I wondered why Maria, our remaining secretary, hadn't brought it in. I also glanced at my phone; the message light wasn't on. I uncrumpled the paper and read the words, "Surgelato ASAP."

Gayle was staring at the door. Felix wasn't particularly handsome, but I'd seen more than one woman stare at the door for a distracted moment after Felix exited. I'd seen Matthilde Warneke do it, as a matter of fact.

Manuel nudged Gayle back to her story. "Is it the kind of thing Julian Warneke might have done, do you think?"

"Put a gun into Martin's briefcase?" Gayle Halberstam sighed. "I worked for him for fourteen wonderful, crazy months, but how do you judge something like that? I always thought Julian was the one with the principles, you know, the real commitment! He used to tell Martin all the time that the courtroom was their podium and that clients hired them to make a political statement!"

"What did Rittenhaus think?"

"He wanted to keep the clients out of jail, that's all. But Julian," she spoke with reverence, "he used to say there were twenty thousand lawyers in the Bay Area, and if that's all their clients wanted, they'd have gone to someone else."

She stood up suddenly, murmuring something about her babysitter. One minute she was there and the next minute she was gone, and but for the presence of Manuel Boyd slouching in my padded vinyl chair, I might have doubted the interview had ever taken place.

I stared across my desk at him. "Not much of a story. She saw Warneke close Rittenhaus's briefcase."

"On March nineteenth."

I smoothed out my pink telephone slip. "Will you excuse me a second?"

I dialed Homicide and asked for the lieutenant. It was the first time I could recall being disappointed to hear he wasn't available. I said I'd call back.

Manuel Boyd's eyes were closed. He tilted his head from one side to the other, apparently trying to work some tension out of his neck; the new career was definitely not agreeing with him. He opened his eyes again. "Is it true what she said about Warneke? That he didn't care about keeping his clients out of jail?"

I nodded. "Yes. But they knew that when they hired him." I remembered the body odor and tobacco smell of the Hall of Justice elevator, the special one leading up to the jail. Maybe I should have admired my parents' commitment, but every time I'd stepped into that elevator, I'd resented them.

"So Gayle was right about that."

"Yes."

"And Pryce, from what I remember of him, was into guerrilla theater—grand, dramatic gestures. Maybe Warneke was just trying to give him the means—"

"To make a political statement with a gun?" I looked at my rumpled telephone message: *Surgelato ASAP.* What did he want? "Julian wasn't that crazy."

"Pryce was working on a book, wasn't he? About

prisoner abuse? Maybe Warneke asked Rittenhaus to give Pryce the tape recorder to help him with his writing."

"Too risky. Julian wouldn't put his own law partner in jeopardy."

Manuel flipped through a tiny spiral notebook. "I did some research. According to old *Chronicle* articles," he smiled when I snorted my contempt for the morning paper, "prisoners conferred with their lawyers in private rooms. Guards stood outside and watched through soundproofed glass. The guard said he saw Rittenhaus hand Pryce a tape recorder, and he saw Pryce fiddle with it. Pryce didn't try to take the tape recorder out of the room, though. What happened was, two other guards thought Pryce was acting funny during his strip search. They said he acted like he was trying to balance something on his head. When the guard reached up to pat Pryce's Afro—"

"Pryce must have known they'd search his wig," I objected. I remembered Pryce's impressive, trademark Afro, how disillusioned I'd been to learn it was a wig.

"Apparently Pryce's Afro was real—up till then. Nobody knows when he cut off his hair or how he got the wig. Obviously he did it some time before Rittenhaus's visit. Anyway, the guards didn't usually check his hair. And this time, when they tried to, Pryce supposedly pulled the gun out from under it." He blinked at his notes. "That's what they claimed. But the main thing is, Pryce didn't take the tape recorder with him, so if things had gone right, no one could possibly have connected Rittenhaus with the gun."

" 'If things had gone right!' What are the odds of successfully hiding a gun under a wig? Julian wouldn't have dropped his partner into a sure-loser of a plan like that!"

"It was a twenty-two, yay big." Manuel stretched his fingers about six inches. "Like the little gun the First Lady packs in her purse."

"So what are you saying? That Martin Rittenhaus came

out of hiding after sixteen years to take revenge on Julian for a plan gone awry?" It was so preposterous I expected Manuel to deny it.

He didn't. He shrugged his bony shoulders. "A person's appearance changes as he gets older. Especially if he shaves off a full beard. Maybe Rittenhaus looks different enough to come back to the city and—"

"Put a hemlock rosette on an amaretto mousse? What kind of half-assed revenge is that?"

"From smuggled guns to amaretto mousse—from radicalism to René's!" Manuel smiled wistfully. "I guess it's too good a story to be true!"

• CHAPTER TWENTY-SIX •

I took a cab to the Hall of Justice. The neighborhood is starkly without foliage, full of drab warehouses and garages. Elevated freeways straddle the streets, blocking light and filling the air with the din of rushing cars, the stench of exhaust. The Hall itself is a big gray box, its drabness accented by a metal sculpture resembling worms on a two-story jungle gym. Across the street, bail-bond companies and criminal lawyers advertise their services in flaked letters on grimy windows. The Line Up bar blinks with dancing neon toros.

I walked through the Hall of Justice metal detector and crossed the orange marble lobby, relieved not to be taking the familiar hallway to the criminal courts. (My mother had cried every time they'd sentenced her; why had she let it happen over and over again?) I rode the elevator to the fourth floor.

Room 450, Homicide, was a madhouse. Uniformed cops and plainclothes inspectors bustled around paired desks in the big common room. Reporters, some with cameras resting on their shoulders, slouched against the wall near the door, glancing at Lieutenant Surgelato's closed door. I spotted Krisbaum, the sloppy detective who'd been asked to babysit me at my office. He appeared to be staring out a huge window at the panorama of elevated freeway traffic. I worked my way across the room to him. No one tried to stop me; no one asked me my business. I could have picked up a stack of case files and walked out with them, I think.

I asked Krisbaum twice if I could see the lieutenant. It

wasn't until I tapped Krisbaum's shoulder that he noticed me. He took a tiny earphone out of his ear and clicked off the tape recorder that was attached to it. After a distracted glance at a sobbing black man who was being escorted into an interrogation room, he pointed to the lieutenant's door. "Go ahead and knock," he shrugged.

Surgelato said, "Come in," so I did. He obviously wasn't expecting me; he stood up and gaped.

This made him look rather foolish, an effect enhanced by an unbuttoned collar, a loosened tie, disheveled hair, and several hours' growth on his chin. Stacks of files, glossy black-and-white photographs, and empty styrofoam cups, each containing a tiny plastic swizzle stick, littered his desk. Behind the desk was a wall of diplomas, commendations, awards, and framed photographs. One photograph I remembered from an earlier visit: it showed a much-younger Surgelato laughing as a crush of football players poured champagne over his head.

"I don't suppose you'd like to take me to René's for lunch?" I ventured.

The lieutenant blinked a few times, then frowned.

"Is this a *faux pas*? Cops don't eat at the scene of the crime?"

His jaw muscles rippled.

"Ah! Not with suspect number one! I get it!" I put my hands on his desktop and leaned toward him. "I do have a police-business reason for wanting to go there with you, though."

He buttoned his top button, fixed his tie, and ran a beefy hand over his coarse black hair. "Come on," he snapped.

He walked right by me, and I followed like a good Arab wife.

I followed him back into room 450 and out through a side door. I followed him through a cheerless beige corridor and into an elevator labeled Authorized Personnel Only. I followed him through an underground parking garage filled with black-and-white SFPD cars.

The lieutenant held open a car door for me. It was an unmarked car, maroon, as big as a boat. When he climbed into the driver's seat, I observed, "You should talk to whoever buys your cars."

"Yeah? What's wrong with this one?" He laid scratch leaving the garage.

"It must be an incredible gas hog and it's ugly as—"

"This happens to be *my* car." He looked at me. "My own personal car, which I got a very good deal on."

"Oh."

He stopped at a light, turning to me. In the shadow of a freeway overpass, I examined him. He was forty-five years old, or thereabouts—maybe ten years older than me. He was short—five-nine, tops—but a good six inches taller than me. His head was big and square, growing out of a thick, short neck. His nose looked like it had sustained several batterings, and his browbone obtruded over small, black eyes, close set. His mouth was narrow but full, almost cupidlike, above the cleft chin that was virtually his only good feature. He had the pale yellow skin of a Mediterranean who'd spent too much time under fluorescent light, and his five o'clock shadow was already in evidence at noon.

"What the hell's this all about?" he demanded, with his usual charm.

"It's a long story, and it involves René's, and I happen to be very hungry."

He looked at me mistrustfully. "Are you serious?"

His attitude was beginning to irritate me. "You've probably asked me out fifty times. Now I suggest you take me to lunch and you act like I'm offering you a contaminated needle!"

"Take you to lunch?" He eyed me with greater approval. "Okay, fine. But why René's? What do you think the reporters in this town would say if they saw us—?" A BMW pulled up behind us and began to honk. Surgelato reacted with an Italian gesture.

The driver leaned on his horn and returned the gesture. Then he pulled into the lane reserved for cross traffic and began swearing at Surgelato as he lowered the passenger window.

Surgelato fumbled in the lapel pocket of his rumpled brown suit. From it he produced a plastic folder with his badge and picture ID. He flashed it at the driver.

The man's expression changed immediately. He hit the button to reraise the window, reversed the car, and got back into the proper lane, behind us.

Surgelato put the badge away, making no attempt to drive through the green light.

"You can't be seen with me," I concluded.

"Not at René's! Jesus! How about some Italian food instead?"

"Okay. But give the BMW a break and drive."

• CHAPTER TWENTY-SEVEN •

Valente's is a small place on Jackson, sufficiently undiscovered that a cop can dine there with his chief suspect and not end up in the morning paper. I had fettuccine dripping with buttery Alfredo.

"If I ate here often I'd be fat as a—"

"Watch it," Surgelato interrupted. "I do eat here often."

"No Italian wife?"

"Had one once. She couldn't cook worth a damn."

"What happened to her?"

"She's around. Finishing a doctorate in abnormal psychology."

"She leave you for someone more abnormal?"

He dunked his French bread into minestrone. "I left her, as a matter of fact."

I wanted to ask why, but I am not completely without manners. Luckily, Surgelato volunteered the information.

"Maybe it was my fault. I don't know. I got it into my head that she was—how can I put it? Not shallow, exactly; 'insincere' is a better word, maybe. At home she was fine. Then we'd go out and she'd be a different person, talking for effect—whatever put her in the spotlight, whatever amused the crowd, you know? Didn't matter if it was true, didn't matter if it hurt me—" He went back to his soup, looking uncomfortable. "I hate that kind of cocktail party charm."

"No kids?"

"Nope. How about you? When we were wrapping up that law school thing, I had the impression you and that guy—"

"We had a big fight. He wasn't faithful." It was my turn to be embarrassed. "I guess you're surprised that matters to me?"

"No. Why should I be surprised?"

"It's not a very hip attitude."

He smiled, looked like he was going to say something, then buttered some more French bread instead.

"I seem to be becoming less hip every day." I pushed away my fettuccine.

"Come on. The good old days, the late sixties— I had to drive a marked unit around the Haight. My personal unpopularity aside, what I used to hear was a bunch of moronic stuff about love and zodiacs and everyone being connected by molecules of space and—god, who even remembers the half of it? Young people weren't thinking—no, no, I know some were—but I mean as a general fashion. I grew up in North Beach. I used to listen to Larry Ferlinghetti read poetry, I had espresso once with Lenny Bruce when I was a kid. I mean, if anything, people used to think too much in the early sixties; then, wham it's the Summer of Love and everyone's into flower power." He grinned. "*Flower* power!"

"It got sappy," I conceded. "But at least we weren't obsessed by our résumés. We cared about civil rights and equal protection, and we'd never have stood for mandatory on-the-job drug testing. I mean, there were actually things people wouldn't put up with for money, back then."

"Jobs are harder to come by these days."

"If you want big bucks, sure. But people didn't care so much about money—"

"College students didn't *have* to care."

"Oh, come on. I worked my way through college, too."

" 'Too?' " His smile was sardonic. "I didn't work a day in my life until I became a cop. Unless you count playing ball."

I looked at his suit; it was hard to believe he'd grown up with money. It's no substitute for taste, I suppose.

Surgelato glanced at his watch. "I gotta get back. You had something to tell me?"

"Yes. Only—" I let the waiter clear our lunch plates. "I promised the woman who told me that I wouldn't go to the pigs with it."

"The pigs. Nice."

"Her phrase. The point is, I'm breaking a promise."

"Screw the promise. This is a murder case."

"And it's kind of crazy." I blushed; it occurred to me that the information wasn't the main thing. I'd wanted company for lunch.

He misinterpreted the blush. "Hey," he said softly. "Really, you're doing the right thing. There are circumstances where you just can't keep a confidence. This is one of them. Somebody's killing people. They might kill you next. They might kill someone you love."

I told him what Gayle Halberstam had said about Julian Warneke being in Martin Rittenhaus's office. I explained Manuel Boyd's wishful interpretation of the episode.

I half expected Surgelato to burst into derisive guffaws. Instead he nodded solemnly. "We've thought of Rittenhaus. 'Wanted and dangerous,' like the poster says. We're not ruling out an old feud."

"But in *The Night of March Nineteenth*—"

"Rittenhaus and Warneke were practically blood brothers. I know." He shook his head. "I'm not saying they weren't, but I'll tell you, it pains me to hear people call that film a documentary. It's a forty-minute commercial for Rittenhaus, and that's all it is." He rolled a crust of French bread along the tabletop. "But tell me something? Why'd you want to tell me this in person? And why at René's, in particular?"

"To see if any of the waiters looked like Martin Rittenhaus."

He grinned. "If Rittenhaus hasn't had plastic surgery, he's a goddam fool."

He dropped a twenty onto the table and stood up.

"No police expense account, Lieutenant?"

"If I pay, I can think of this as a date. It's worth twenty to my ego."

As there was no hint of overbearing jock in his manner, I decided to think of it that way, too. And thinking of it that way, I forgot to ask Surgelato why he'd left a message for me to call him.

• CHAPTER TWENTY-EIGHT •

I'd used up all my objections, both peremptory and for cause, and still ended up with a jury that would have made Daniel Webster shudder. I tried to make my client understand this.

The boy was only nineteen. At nineteen, I'd felt like an adult; maybe the boy felt that way, too. But his cheeks were chubby, he blushed violently without provocation, and his ideas were straight out of Marxism 101.

"Fifteen years ago," I told him, "Judge Rondi gave me sixty days for doing almost nothing. Two military policemen were carrying me off government property, and I told one of them to go fuck himself." I caught myself about to ravage my hair. "I could have said any number of things to Judge Rondi. I could have apologized. I could have claimed I didn't know what I was saying, that the MPs misinterpreted me, that I meant no disrespect—you get the picture?"

The boy regarded me sullenly.

"Okay, but instead of doing that, I let my lawyer argue freedom of speech. He delivered this lecture about the word 'fuck' and its political importance as a symbol of resistance. I thought it was great at the time; it was exactly what I believed myself. But it made Judge Rondi furious. Every time my lawyer said 'fuck,' Rondi hit the ceiling. And the way things worked out, of the seventy-plus demonstrators who were arrested with me, only *I* got jail time."

"I don't mind going to jail for what I believe in."

"But you shouldn't have to go to jail. You *don't* have to."

I heard an echo of desperation in my voice; how many times had I said this very thing to my parents? "If you do go to jail, they've got you. You've delivered yourself to them. You've let them win."

He shook his head. "They win if I let them dictate my behavior."

"What do you think they do in jail? They get you up at six, herd you into group showers, feed you cold mush, make you do some dumb, tedious job all day, strip search you every time you have visitors. You have no privacy, no time to yourself. I mean, they've *got* you."

And the boy confirmed what Julian Warneke had always believed about our clients. "If I wanted a bunch of co-opted bullshit from my lawyer, I'd have gone to my dad."

"I just want you to know what you're getting yourself into. There's no draft right now. Registering with the selective service doesn't put you at risk. If you go down and register tomorrow morning before trial, I'll move to dismiss the charges against you. The U.S. Attorney will go for it, I'm sure. And if the government does reinstitute the draft someday, you can resist *then*, when it really matters."

He flushed in damp patches. "It matters now. I don't have to wait until I'm personally threatened before I refuse to acquiesce to an unjust law!" When he shook his head, his cheeks trembled. "I came here because I heard you guys had principles!"

I'd heard my parents express similar sentiments a thousand times. And yet, I looked at the boy and was conscious of a growing dislike for him; if he *really* understood the consequences, maybe he'd be less anxious for the show. A voice in my head told me I'd once have thought him principled and brave, but that was before my metamorphosis into a crank. "Okay, look, you hired me, and I've given you my advice. Now it's up to you. I'll do what you want. As long as you understand your options."

"No deals. I want a trial. I want to tell the world why I did it." He wiped a glaze of sweat from his cheeks.

I spent two hours with him, going over his testimony. By the time he left, my hair was in twisted, multidirectional tangles. He was going to say what he wanted and the hell with me. When I closed my eyes I could see the Honorable Manolo M. Rondi up on the bench, his black robe emphasizing the floridity of his cheeks, his eyes glinting like slivers of obsidian, and his mouth twisted with disgust.

I phoned Bill Ingram. "Do you have a copy of *March Nineteenth* I could borrow?"

"Sure." There was an arrogant purr in his voice. "Do you have a videocassette recorder?"

"My landlord does."

"I'm on my way downtown. I can drop it by your office, if you're still there. You know," he added, "my agent's negotiating a deal with the studio—they're talking about colorizing it and splicing it with fictionalized reenactments for a TV docudrama. They're talking Jeff Goldblum for the lead."

I hung up and wandered over to Felix's office to ask him a question about my trial. I found him hunched over his computer with Clement Kerrey, typing numbers onto the screen. Both men looked pleased.

They glanced up simultaneously when I walked in, then turned back to the screen, displaying no interest in me. "Teamster retainers?" I deduced.

Clement smiled toothily. "A twenty-five percent increase—that'll keep our prices well below what our competitors charge, but we'll be doing fine!" He clapped Felix's back, and Felix grinned at the screen.

"Will the Teamsters go for it?"

Clement nodded, still admiring the numbers. "Semi will; he grouses about our fee, but he knows we've been undercharging him. Hank might take some persuading. One hundred and fifty-four will go for it, I think. I don't anticipate any problems with our other locals."

I asked Felix my question, but he was too preoccupied to answer me. Clement pulled a pen out of his shirt pocket and wrote down the appropriate federal rule numbers, right off the top of his head. I was impressed. I rewarded him with an account of Bill Ingram's plan for *The Night of March Nineteenth*. "A colorized docudrama! Can you believe it?"

Clement nodded. "Ingram represented the studio when it locked out its writers." Representing management: any subsequent perfidy might be expected.

Felix just smiled and kept on crunching numbers. I noticed a familiar face staring up at me from a software catalog on Felix's desk. "*Mind Mirror*, by Timothy Leary!" the catalog announced. "The newest route to cerebral stimulation! Get high on high tech!"

• CHAPTER TWENTY-NINE •

Ben Bubniak dozed on a Victorian couch he'd inherited from his mother. His head was wedged between the carved wood arm and the button-studded back. Falling from his hand was a copy of *The Great-Great-Great-Grandchildren of Dune* (or something to that effect). I smoked a joint and watched *The Night of March Nineteenth* on his TV.

The film began in *Untouchables* black and white: police cars streaming through the gates of Folsom prison, the warden climbing out of a car, a camera-eye rushing through cell blocks, men in suits huddling, a black woman crying in the arms of an older woman, a shot of Martin Rittenhaus's empty office. Ingram had obviously pulled together footage from many different sources, and I had to admit he'd done it expertly. (Would he really let a TV studio colorize it?)

Suddenly, the warden was making an announcement; the sound quality was poor, the film washed out, the camera tilted slightly—all to excellent effect. Harlen Pryce had been discovered to possess a loaded firearm and had been shot and killed in the "process of his disarmament." The camera seemed to reel with shock. A warrant had issued for the arrest of Pryce's lawyer, Martin S. Rittenhaus. Evidence indicated that the twenty-two caliber firearm had been smuggled to Pryce by Rittenhaus inside Rittenhaus's tape recorder, which Rittenhaus had carried into the prison in his briefcase. In the future, all lawyers would be carefully searched.

The film switched to a double profile. Home movies and

news footage of Pryce were interspersed with footage about Rittenhaus, his middle-class roots, rallies he'd organized at his law school (which happened to be the same one I'd attended), films of him outside various courtrooms, commenting on the trials of some of his notorious clients, including Harlen Pryce.

Then, interviews with Rittenhaus's friends, including Julian Warneke. It was a jolt seeing Julian there, sixteen years younger, his hair darker, his skin unlined, talking about his law partner until tears began rolling down his cheeks and he could no longer control the contortions of his mouth.

I started to cry, too, not for Rittenhaus—I'd never known him; he'd gone underground while I was still in Boston. I cried for Julian. For political ideals that had put many a willing body into jail, for a protest movement that had lost momentum before Ronald Reagan and his mandatory drug tests, his gutting of civil rights and labor laws. I cried because I'd grown to resent Julian Warneke as much as I'd once admired him: I'd grown to resent his underpaying me, his part in putting me in jail, and even his choice of restaurants.

I cried to the background music of Joan Baez singing "Carry it on, carry it on . . ." Her voice faded into that of less talented singers, less talented guitarists, tunelessly but enthusiastically singing the same song.

A faint thumping sound startled me. I looked at Ben's television. Martin Rittenhaus, tall and slumped, with his wild bush of brown hair and big horn-rimmed glasses sliding down his small nose, sat in front of the campanile at Berkeley, singing in a circle of students.

I looked at the screen and gasped. Sitting on his left was Kit Kline, former Trotskyite, now business agent for Teamsters Local 16.

Ben's book dropped from his hand, startling him awake. "What?" he yawned. "Are we still watching this? Did you say something, Earth Woman?"

"I'm scared."

He sat up, his pale face puffy with sleep. "You should be scared. We should all be scared. The Second Coming is a scary proposition!"

I turned off the television and rewound the film. I could feel my heart pounding in the veins of my neck. Don, I thought, be there, be there.

• CHAPTER THIRTY •

"**T**his is Willa Jansson. May I speak to Lieutenant Surgelato?"

"One moment."

An unmelodic voice came on the line. "Krisbaum," it announced. The slovenly inspector. "What can I do you for, Miss Jansson?"

"I'd like to talk to the lieutenant."

"Talk to me. I can help you."

I supposed it was no use making a fetish of talking to the Big Man himself. But I was conscious of my disappointment. "I think I know where you can get some information about Martin Rittenhaus. Maybe. I'm not sure."

"Rittenhaus?" Judging from the series of clunking sounds, Krisbaum had dropped the receiver. He came back on the line. "What kind of information?"

"I don't know. It's just this coincidental thing. I don't know how important it is."

"What is it?"

I told him about Kit Kline, that he'd been at Caesar's Tahoe when Mae died, that he'd pulled a gun on me there. "Kline was a political ally of a Teamster named Jim Zissner who might also have been murdered— Oh, never mind that. The point is, I just saw him sitting next to Martin Rittenhaus—"

"*What!* You saw Rittenhaus?"

"Not in person. In the final scene of *The Night of March Nineteenth*. You know, that movie about—"

"Yeah, I know. Hold on." I thought I heard the lieutenant's voice in the background. I expected Krisbaum to put him on the line, but he didn't. He said, "Okay, Miss Jansson. We'll check it out."

I hung up, troubled by an unpleasant suspicion.

I picked up the phone again, dialed Homicide again. This time I identified myself as Matthilde Warneke. "May I speak to Lieutenant Surgelato, please?"

"One moment."

And he came on the line, the bastard. "Surgelato here. Hello? Mrs. Warneke?"

I hung up. Put my hands on my cheeks to cool them. Surgelato didn't want to talk to me, didn't want to deal with me anymore; he'd assigned Krisbaum to babysit me again.

I'd gone to his office; I'd asked him to lunch; he'd been seen fraternizing with suspect number one. If the *Chronicle* was any indication, the lieutenant was already getting bad press; multiple murders will do that. I supposed he couldn't afford any gossip.

But, Jesus, to refuse to talk to me when I needed to—

My god! Needed to talk to a cop? What was happening to me?

• CHAPTER THIRTY-ONE •

I walked to Manuel Boyd's place, a high-ceilinged, wainscoted flat not far from that last vestige of the sixties, the Haight-Ashbury Free Clinic (*By appointment only! No drop-ins!* read the sign on the clinic door).

Manuel looked tired, but he didn't seem especially surprised to see me. He wore a Giants sweatshirt and sweatpants so big the drawstring was wrapped twice around his waist. The apartment was much as I remembered it, reasonably tidy, with a sectional couch, a huge coffee table, a lot of crowded bookcases, and not much else.

"How long has it been since you've seen *The Night of March Nineteenth*?"

"I saw it yesterday." Manuel sat perfectly still on the couch, his head sunk into the cushions.

"In the last scene, Rittenhaus is singing in a group—"

"'Carry It On.'"

"There's a man sitting on his left—"

"Kline? With the guitar?"

"You *know* him?"

"A woman I used to know identified him for me. Him and some other people in that group." He closed his eyes for a moment, discreetly massaging his stomach. "She's an interesting woman. Maybe the most interesting woman I know."

"You don't know where Kline lives, do you?"

"How come?"

"I've known him for years." I was ashamed of myself

and hoped I didn't look it. "I just found out the cops are looking for him, to talk to him about something that happened at a Teamsters conference last week. I thought I'd let him know."

Manuel frowned. I felt sleazy, lying to him; sleazy, having sicced the police on Kline.

I brooded about it in the cab. The driver kept turning around to look at me. I didn't tip him; Pavlovian conditioning not to ogle blondes.

Kline lived in the Noe Valley, on a winding loop of road atop Portrero Hill. From his front door I could see the lighted windows of a hundred modest houses, arranged on the hillside like Christmas tree lights. Kline's house needed paint almost as badly as his weedy lawn needed cutting. Interior lights shone through sagging front curtains. I could hear the piercing "no no NO" of a young child.

Kline answered the door himself. He was unshaven and shirtless, with a V-neck sweater pulled over his skinny, hairless chest. His unbelted jeans hung low on his hipbones and he was barefoot. I'd made love to many a man wearing just such an outfit; maybe that's why I found it repulsive.

He laughed when he saw me. "Oh, Jesus, what's it going to be? The riot act? A punch in the nose? Another lecture about the Noble Teamster?"

Somewhere in the house, the child burst into squeaky, tuneless song. Kline smiled.

"I want to talk to you about Martin Rittenhaus."

The smile vanished. He led me through a hallway littered with tiny trucks, some of them in the throes of becoming robots. We passed what was obviously a child's bedroom. A woman in a polyester shirt, tight pants, and high heels struggled to quell the singing toddler. Over his shoulder, Kline commented, "A born troublemaker, like his mom!"

The living room looked like an ad for Sears' bargain

basement. It was cheap and immaculate. It was the last thing in the world I'd have imagined of Kline.

I sat on plaid Herculon, wondering what the hell I was trying to accomplish. I'd called the cops; I shouldn't have, but I had. What good would it do, talking to Kline myself?

Kline picked up a half-empty bottle of beer. "Rittenhaus," he prompted me.

"I just saw *The Night of March Nineteenth*."

"Yeah?"

"You're in that last scene with him."

Kline nodded. "Most inspiring son of a bitch I ever met."

"Why'd you pull a gun on me at the joint council, Kit?"

Kline chugalugged the rest of the bottle, then smacked his lips. Macho Teamster.

"Look, Kit, I heard that business agent from Local 92, that TDU guy, say 'nice work' to you. What did he mean?"

"Bailey?" Kline chuckled. "He hates your fucking law firm. Probably happy to see me pull a gun on you. Prob'ly you annoyed him. You always were the most fucking annoying person at every meeting—"

"*I* was?" *You* say that? When you used to—" The toddler's wail startled me into silence.

Kline, apparently used to the sound, ignored it. "Know what's wrong with you? You're a cynic. You don't believe anything's gonna do any good. You don't believe it about the Teamsters for a Democratic Union. You didn't used to believe it about—"

"The Trotskyites' precious general strike? The country reelects Richard Nixon by a landslide, and you're trying to organize a general strike!"

"You didn't like anybody's ideas! You were like a goddam kid who got dragged to Sunday school by her parents." He waved his empty bottle. "No matter what anybody suggested, you thought it was crap."

I grabbed a fistful of my hair. "We were in the middle of a

war and instead of focusing on that, everybody wanted to picket the damn utility company or dress up like Native Americans and march to City Hall. I mean, empty gestures are easy. Symbolism is easy. Being effective isn't. I just wanted to stick to the point."

"Oh, stick to the point! Sure!" Kline belched. "The fucking narrowest little point you could define! The war was a symptom of something a lot bigger than—"

I stood up. "God! God damn it! Get two lefties together in a room and it always turns into a cockfight! It's no wonder Reagan—" I took a few deep breaths. Sat back down. "You're saying you pulled a gun on me because you resent my political views? Well, your little stunt's bound to cost TDU the election. And I don't believe you're that dumb. You're Semi Sawyer's man, aren't you? You were cinching the election for him, weren't you?"

Kline thumped down the bottle. "Why don't you get the hell out of here."

"What's in it for you, Kit? What did Sawyer buy you with? Or don't you care enough about the union to give a damn *who* runs it?"

"I said, get the fuck out of here!" His hair fell over his brow, and his hand shook slightly as he brushed it back. His toddler was quiet now, I could hear the click of a woman's heels in the hallway.

"Do you know where Martin Rittenhaus is?"

Kline's lip twitched; I thought for a second he was going to smile.

Then the high-heeled woman appeared at the living room door. Her eyes, caked with blue makeup, were open wide, and her face was so pale her rouge stood out like a clown's. "Kit," she said. "Police."

And sure enough, standing right behind her was Inspector Krisbaum, his too-short tie askew and his shirt unbuttoned at the belly. He held his hat in one hand and his badge ID in the other.

As he extended the latter to Kline, he frowned at me. It was the kind of frown that promises a major explosion, after the company's gone.

"Like to ask you a few questions, Mr. Kline."

Kline exchanged glances with the woman. She shook her head almost imperceptibly, her stiffly sprayed pageboy hardly moving.

Kline said, "I don't have to talk to you."

"We're investigating the murders of Julian Warneke and Mae Siegel, and we think you might to be able to help us, Mr. Kline. You don't have to talk to us, but we'd certainly appreciate your cooperation."

"My cooperation?" He shook his head.

Krisbaum looked at me with cold fury.

Again, he requested Kline's cooperation; again, Kline shook his head.

On his way out, Krisbaum said to me, "I don't know what you're playing at, Miss Jansson, but God damn it!"

As soon as he was gone, Kline grabbed my arm and jerked me out of my chair. "Did you call the cops on me?"

I didn't answer.

"Get the hell out of my house!"

I stepped past the polyestered woman, her perfume hitting me like tear gas. I lingered in the hallway long enough to avoid encountering Krisbaum on the porch, then I walked downhill until I found a telephone. I called a cab to take me home.

One thing for sure, I'd be hearing from Surgelato now.

• CHAPTER THIRTY-TWO •

The jury, following the letter of the law, found my client guilty.

I heard the commotion behind me in the pewlike seats, but I was thinking about my own trial. Judge Rondi had a habit of leaning back in his leather chair so that from below you saw only a cliff of oak bench. I'd listened to Julian Warneke plead my case, and I'd wondered if there was anyone up there to hear it. Today, pleading the boy's case, I'd noticed myself stepping farther and farther back until I stood at the spectators' rail, trying to catch a glimpse of the judge. A few times Rondi had leaned forward to overrule my objections; he'd pushed aside his copy of my brief as if the paper itself offended him. On his face, I'd seen the same disdainful anger that had once sentenced me to sixty days in jail.

The boy could get as much as five years.

I was conscious of a chant growing up in the courtroom. My client joined in it. I whispered to him, "He still hasn't sentenced you! Don't antagonize him!"

The boy stepped away from me, chanting louder. The chant was, "Hell no, we won't go!" Rondi didn't try to speak over it; he simply motioned to the federal marshal.

The marshal glanced at me as he handcuffed the boy's hands behind his back. Rondi was saying, "—contempt of court."

Over the din, I heard him thank and dismiss the jurors. They filed past the bench; a few of them glanced back at the crowd, looking a little frightened. A federal court clerk in a navy blue suit held open a door for them, smiling and speaking a few pleasant words to each. The clerk then ordered us to rise, and the judge exited through the same door, his black robe billowing like Dracula's cape.

The marshal checked to make sure that the handcuffs were secure. Then he said, "Come on, son." The boy looked flushed and victorious; he didn't speak to me as he walked past.

I gathered up my papers. I thought I heard someone in the pews compliment me on my closing argument. I turned around, trying to focus on that person. I considered voicing my outrage; my argument had been what the boy had wanted, and it had been the best I could do under the circumstances, but it had doomed my client to jail. I'd asked the jury to ignore the law, to make a political statement; it's a rare and unconscientious jury that will do that.

I left the courtroom, walking conspicuously down the aisle like a jilted bride. I stepped into the cool, gray-carpeted hallway. Once the massive door closed behind me, the only sound I heard was the murmur of air-conditioning. A federal clerk strode by me, dignified even in haste.

Then the courtroom door opened and a squeaky voice wailed, "Baby! That poor boy! You were wonderful!"

I was engulfed in a weeping bundle of proud motherhood. I closed my eyes and let my mother praise me; I needed the embrace, however ridiculous I thought the congratulations.

When I opened my eyes, I saw Don Surgelato standing to Mother's left, his hands in his trouser pockets, his expression somewhere between contemptuous and disgusted.

I backed out of Mother's arms. I bumped into a man who identified himself as a reporter from the *Examiner*.

I turned to him, startled. Out of the corner of my eye, I

saw my father step up beside Mother and quietly begin to shush her.

The reporter asked me a question. I didn't understand it; I shook my head. I looked at the lieutenant again. And I learned something; not from the expression on his face, but from the pain it caused me.

I walked blindly to the elevator and punched the down button. My client would be in the prisoners' elevator by now. I remembered it all too well. I could hear the crowd spilling out of the courtroom, and was grateful when the elevator doors opened.

I stepped inside, hit the express-down button, then the door-close button. But I wasn't fast enough. Surgelato stuck a wing-tipped foot between the closing doors. They reopened, and he slid in quickly, hitting the door-close button before anyone else could join us.

"Warneke would have been proud of you," he commented.

I didn't reply.

"Kid'll get, what? two, three years, you figure? U.S. Attorney had to do some finagling to get Judge Rondi, I heard. But he says it was worth it; that his case was in the bag the minute you decided not to cut a deal."

I stared at my pumps. Mother had scuffed the toes.

"Christ, Willa! Was that the best you could do for that kid?"

The elevator doors opened and I walked through them.

Surgelato accompanied me through the bustling lobby. I cleared my throat, tested my voice. "Do you want to ask me some questions? Is that why you're here?"

"I wanted to watch you work." He shook his head slightly. "But, yeah. Krisbaum's got some questions for you. Drop by the Hall later."

He pushed open a glass door for me, and I ran down the broad, shallow steps of the federal building. I walked several blocks before turning to make sure Surgelato was no longer behind me.

Krisbaum had some questions for me. Krisbaum. I supposed it shouldn't matter who I talked to: a cop was a cop.

• CHAPTER THIRTY-THREE •

Felix Flish stepped into my office and folded his long body into a chair. "So, the client got what he wanted."

"Yes."

He patted my hand. "Well, look, if he wants to be a symbol of—"

"Why did he have to involve me? I feel like a pimp for the federal marshal."

"You've had a rough month, all around. Clement says some TDU guy pulled a gun on you at the joint council."

"That was comic relief, compared to the other stuff that's been going on."

"I had a guy pull a gun on me once in law school. I was in line to get some lunch and he was sitting at one of the tables beside the line. Not a student, just a wino off the street, a nut. The thing wasn't loaded, thank god. And security hustled him right out of the building. But I didn't much care for it, and that's the truth."

"It's no fun," I agreed, turning my face away. A wino? At Stanford Law School? In my four undergrad years at Stanford, I'd never once seen a wino on that posh campus. What was Felix trying to prove with his fabricated bit of commiseration?

"Well, I'm out of here. I've got my car, if you want a lift home."

I remembered riding with Felix to Julian's wake, a Rolling Stones tape blasting out my eardrums. "No thanks."

I took the streetcar to my parents' house. I didn't relish discussing the trial with them, but I didn't want to be alone with my thoughts, either.

And as for Krisbaum, if he really wanted me, he could come and find me.

• CHAPTER THIRTY-FOUR •

My father suffers from the delusion that he can make tofu taste like meat. I've probably had two hundred different tofu dishes in my life, and none of them has tasted even remotely like meat. Tofu never really tastes like much of anything, in fact; it's more of a texture than a flavor. But who was I to tell my father that his oasis of veal was a mirage? I told him I could almost hear my dinner mooing.

After dinner, Daddy and I sat at the table drinking coffee while Mother washed the dishes. I could hear her singing "The Green, Green Grass of Home," and probably the upstairs neighbors could, too.

Daddy looked at me and sighed.

"You're not going to start in about my pot habit again, are you? I can't handle criticism unless I'm stoned."

He smiled, but only for a second. "It's none of my business"—an inauspicious start, if ever there was one—"but I hate to see your mother upset."

She was bellowing, "'Down the road I looook, and here comes Mary—'"

"She doesn't sound upset to me."

"She will be if you—" He set his mug down. "It was hard for her, trying to accept your soldier."

"It's not like she bent over backward being gracious to him, Daddy."

"I'm not trying to tell you how to pick your friends,

146

but . . ." He shook his head. "I don't know what she'd say if you brought home a policeman."

Perceptive old goat. "Don't worry about it."

He continued to look worried.

"Daddy, you guys aren't hiding anything, are you? That's not what this is about, is it?"

Mother's song swelled to a crescendo, " 'I wake and look around me, at the cold gray walls that surround me, and I realize that I was only dreaming . . .' "

My father stood up, collecting our empty mugs. "I'd better go help your mother. Before the neighbors complain."

I spent a few more minutes at the table, toying with some crumbs and feeling lousy. When the phone rang, I answered it.

A man's voice said, "June, listen—" Then a pause.

Then a dial tone.

Felix Flish, I was almost certain. The goddam liar didn't know my mother, eh?

I walked out the front door. Felix and Mother were lying to me, and it gave me the creeps. But I was in no mood to call them on it, not tonight.

It was twilight. A cold wind lifted my skirt, stung my face. Across the street, streetlamps flickered blue and orange, struggling to come on.

I turned left, heading home.

A figure at the end of the block stopped and seemed to watch me. Then it turned tail, disappearing swiftly around the corner.

But I'd seen the woman clearly enough to recognize her, in spite of the failing light. She was devoid of makeup, and her hair was brushed into a ponytail at the nape of her neck. She wore a T-shirt and jeans. But I recognized her.

It was Kit Kline's housemate, the woman with the stiff pageboy and the tight polyester clothes, the woman who'd signaled Kline that he was not to answer Krisbaum's questions.

And if she hadn't been on her way to my mother's house, I was a moron (a possibility I could never completely dismiss).

I didn't go home, after all. I walked past the Free Clinic to Manuel Boyd's apartment.

Manuel was packing a small suitcase. He looked exhausted. He had dark circles under his eyes, and his skin was pale even for a San Franciscan's.

"You're going somewhere?"

He dropped onto the couch. "On assignment."

"Oh." We were friends, but not close enough for me to tell him he looked too sick to work. "You told me you'd identified Kline through a woman you used to know. Would you mind telling me who?"

Manuel Boyd paused. "Did you go to Kline's house?"

I nodded. "I was going to tell him the cops wanted to talk to him, and instead we got into a big fight about movement politics. A cop showed up right in the middle of it."

Boyd raised his brows; even this small a display of interest seemed to tax him. He massaged his stomach. "What did Kline do?"

"Kicked the cop out. Does your friend know the woman who lives with Kline?"

Manuel smiled. "So that's it. You recognized her?"

I remembered the woman's blue-caked eyes, the spots of rouge on her cheeks. Even without the makeup, she hadn't looked familiar. "Recognized her? No. Do I know her?"

Manuel Boyd glanced at his suitcase. "I thought you might. Her name's Hillary Jones. She used to be political; I thought you might have known her from those days."

"What else do you know about her?"

"I met her in college. We worked on the paper together. Like I said, she used to be political. That's why I talked to her about *March Nineteenth*." He smiled. "She identified Kline for me. I guess they've been together a while. She mentioned a kid."

"That's all you know about her?"

"Well— I don't mean to be coy, but I don't want to invade her privacy, either."

What the hell did that mean? Since when did reporters worry about invading people's privacy?

He glanced at his suitcase again.

"When will you be back?"

"Soon, I hope. I'm not sure."

At his front door, Manuel did something he'd never done before. He embraced me.

• CHAPTER THIRTY-FIVE •

There was another hate letter in my mailbox. White bond paper, plain white business envelope, neat pica type, the same as two other letters I'd received. Its author once again described how I'd murdered my fellow law students two years earlier—where I'd hidden myself, where I'd hidden my weapons, how I'd connived to make myself seem an intended victim. Floor plans of Malhousie Law School had been published in dozens of newspapers during the trial, but my pen pal had detailed knowledge of classrooms and offices— whether they were kept locked, kept lighted, the kinds of hiding places they contained.

The letter went on to say that this time, the tables would be turned on me. Not that I'd killed Julian, Bess, and Mae; only that I'd be blamed. It gave me the willies.

Maybe it was just coincidence—Julian killed at lunch with me, Bess in the office with me, Mae at the same hotel. Or maybe someone was making sure I was in the vicinity of each murder.

I held the letter up to my reading lamp: Democracy Bond, the watermark informed me. I knew there were ways to determine who'd written a letter; taking fingerprints, matching typeface, analyzing paper. Unfortunately, I had no idea how to do any of those things. I needed an expert.

I knew two experts. Lieutenant Surgelato, the logical choice, seemed to believe I was unprofessional at best, and a murderess at worst.

And the other? Compared to my current problems, herpes seemed like small potatoes. I folded the letters back into their envelopes, tucked them into a manila envelope, and addressed it to Edward Hershey. I enclosed a note asking him to find out who'd written them, if he could. I didn't offer him a fee; I figured he owed me.

I walked down to the corner and dropped the packet into the mailbox for early morning pickup. I was climbing my front stairs when Krisbaum pulled up in a mud-brown Mustang. He motioned to me, leaning over to open the passenger door. I could hear Ben Bubniak's TV blaring, the nine-thousandth rerun of a *MASH* episode.

I stuck my head into the car.

"Didn't the lieutenant mention I had a few questions for you, Miss Jansson?"

"Yes." I glanced back at my apartment building. "I don't suppose we could talk here?"

Krisbaum shook his head. His jowls shook for an extra few seconds, in aftershock. "Got something to show you."

I climbed in.

Krisbaum took me through the Hall of Justice garage and up the police elevator to the roomful of cluttered desks. I tried not to glance at the door to the lieutenant's office as Krisbaum walked me past it. He led me into a room with white cork soundproofing on the walls and ceiling. The room was hardly big enough for a library table and four sturdy chairs. I sat in one of them and watched Krisbaum spread some eight-by-ten glossies on the table. "Do you recognize any persons in these photographs?"

I picked up one of the pictures, adjusting it so it didn't glint fluorescent light at me. It was a still of the final scene of *The Night of March Nineteenth*.

I pointed. "That's Martin Rittenhaus, and this is Kit Kline, playing guitar."

I felt uncomfortable looking at the photograph—not quite scared, but definitely anxious. I remembered being startled out of my tears when the scene had played on Ben's videocassette recorder. I'd looked at the TV, seen Kit Kline, and attributed my unease to him. But now I realized my fear had preceded seeing Kline; it was the reason I'd opened my eyes. I looked at the photograph and re-experienced the feeling without remembering what had brought it on.

What had I psychosynthesized, sitting there in Ben's living room?

"'Carry It On,'" I said aloud.

"Do what?"

"That's the song they're singing. 'Carry It On.'" I shook my head. "We certainly didn't carry it on, did we?"

"Yeah, well, right now I'm not too interested in that. Rittenhaus and Kline. You're sure that's Kline?"

"Yes." My eye strayed to some of the others in the group.

I almost dropped the photograph. It was too absurd; it couldn't be. "Who's this woman? Do you know?"

"She look familiar to you?"

"Like someone who used to be in the news."

"You're right about that. Karen Weillar's her name."

"Rob a bank for peace! The Weillars!" For whom my mother had baked countless banana breads. "This is their daughter."

"Rob a—? Yeah, that's right. Feds got her parents for bank robbery. They think the daughter was driving the getaway car, but the Weillars never made it out of the bank, and the feds never caught up with the daughter."

"I must have seen her picture in the papers."

Her nose was bulbous and her hair was as short as a boy's. But frozen on glossy stock, with her eyes open wide and her lips parted—

What had Surgelato said about Martin Rittenhaus? That he was a damned fool if he hadn't had plastic surgery?

Trim off Karen Weillar's nose, grow out her hair, and dress her in polyester, and unless I was very much mistaken, you'd have Kit Kline's roommate, Hillary Jones.

• CHAPTER THIRTY-SIX •

My apartment door was ajar. I knew I'd left it unlocked when I'd gone to mail the letter to Hershey, but I didn't remember having left it open. I could hear my phone ringing—when had I put it back on the hook?

I dashed up the stairs and threw the door open, reaching the phone just in time to hear a dial tone. I reached out to turn on the reading lamp and froze with my arm extended; my front door had slammed shut. I turned my head. My curtain was open, and the streetlamp outside made a monster shadow of the heap of papers on my table. My front door was lost in that shadow. I said, "Who's there?"

I heard a clicking sound. I'd never heard the sound before, but it frightened me enough to get my legs moving.

I darted into the kitchen. As the door swung shut behind me, it splintered. Some sound must have accompanied it, but all I can remember is looking behind me and being hit in the face with a spray of fuzzy slivers. Seeing a six-inch hole in the door.

I fumbled with my back door; my fingers felt numb and stupid, the way they do when I try to type. I ran down a flight of rickety stairs, past Ben Bubniak's back door. I saw more splintering, the bannister, right in front of me. This time, I heard the cracking sound that accompanied it.

My impulse was to stop, to turn around and get shot and get it over with. I was too scared to keep running.

My brain worked through this paradox quickly, thank

god. I sprinted to the fence separating Ben's weed patch from our Italian neighbor's legume garden. I heard another crack. Nothing around me splintered. I hoped it meant that Whoever was a bad marksman at long range.

Unfortunately, I was equally bad at scaling fences in the dark. My shirt got hung up on a nail, and I all but tore my sleeve off, scrambling over it. Any vague thought of running through dark gardens vanished. As soon as my feet hit Swiss chard, I headed for the breezeway separating my neighbor's building from Ben's. I'd take my chances on the street.

I was fumbling with a rusty slip bolt when I heard footsteps on the street. I stopped, standing very still. The footsteps came closer to the breezeway door. I flattened myself against my neighbor's wall, holding my breath. I could hear streetcar wires buzzing. Inside my neighbor's house, someone coughed.

I imagined I heard that clicking sound again: the hammer of a gun being pulled into cocked position. I remembered the explosion of tiny splinters in my kitchen; my brain showed me a cross-section of the typically flimsy breezeway door.

And then, interior lights came on behind me. I blinked, suddenly caught in a rectangle of light.

Behind and above me, a window opened. A voice rasped, "*Chi è?* Who is there?" I could smell garlic from ten feet below.

From the other side of the breezeway door came an indecisive shuffling of shoes on concrete. Then I heard the footsteps retreat, growing fainter.

I looked up to see my neighbor's round face. "*Mannaggia!*" he commented, looking down at me. "What you do in my yard, *Signorina Avvocatessa?*" Miss Lawyer—he always called me that.

I pressed my hand to my chest; my heart was racing. "I'm sorry I disturbed you, Mr. Cardoni!"

"What's a matter, *Signorina?*"

It was such a long story. And I doubted Mr. Cardoni would like me any the better for it. "I'm looking for my cat."

He scowled. "Ah! So she is *your* cat! Why you don't keep her inside? She sings! All night long she is singing!"

"I'm sorry." Sorry I hadn't invented a better pretext. "When I find her I'll take her inside."

"And she is all the time digging my garden! Her *merda* I find all over!"

I unbolted the breezeway door. "I'll keep her inside. I promise."

I didn't go home, I didn't want to go near the place, under the circumstances. I decided instead to go to my parents' house, to use their phone and demand their sympathy.

I spent as much time looking over my shoulder and listening for footsteps as I did walking. Every sound, every gleam of headlights, sent me running around the nearest corner. A few repetitions of this and I was farther from my parents' apartment than when I started. I cursed myself for not having confided in Mr. Cardoni.

I finally grew too chilled to do more than merely trudge along, trusting to fate. I was too exhausted to think; I guess that's what it took for me to finally psychosynthesize some information into insight.

I stood at the end of my parents' block, staring at the Victorian facade of the apartment building they'd inhabited as long as I could remember. In the diffuse light of the lamp across the street, you couldn't tell that the place needed paint, that the stairs were worn, that the windowsills were beginning to crumble.

Mother's silhouette appeared in the red glow of her front curtains, which she'd hand sewn from Panamanian flags. She seemed to be doing toe touches.

My mother: enlisting in the Peace Corps on her forty-fifth birthday, putting a tiny hammer scar into a missile nose cone, recounting with pride how she'd taught her cell mate to read comic books, organizing car caravans to Watsonville Canning to walk their picket lines, baking tough, floury banana breads for whichever of her friends happened to be in jail. For the Weillars.

She was the last person in the world I could talk to about what had just happened. In fact, I'd be a damned fool to talk to anyone about it, anyone at all.

And I wondered: Did Mother realize what she'd gotten herself into this time?

• CHAPTER THIRTY-SEVEN •

In retrospect, it was probably the stupidest thing I could have done, but then, I'm frequently stupid in retrospect. I needed money, I needed a jacket, and I needed the security of familiar surroundings. I hopped the next streetcar to my office.

I picked up my trench coat, rifled my desk for cash, and wallowed in the familiarness of the place. Malingering was particularly stupid.

I'd underestimated a man who'd eluded government agents for sixteen years, a man who displayed the stamina and audacity to start over again: college, law school (I'd have painted houses before I went through law school again), the bar exam—all for the second time.

I should have known I couldn't outsmart Martin Rittenhaus. The man was a hunted criminal, yet he exercised de facto control over Julian Warneke's law firm. He was sleeping with Julian's wife, and through my mother—the bleeding-heart steward of a secret trust—he would eventually control Julian's fortune, too.

Julian must have felt he owed Martin the partnership and the house; he'd put a gun into Martin's briefcase the morning of March nineteenth, triggering the bloody murder of Harlen Pryce, and driving an innocent man underground. But there's more than one way to force your partner underground, and Rittenhaus's way had been decidedly more permanent.

Julian Warneke had served his purpose: he'd made Rittenhaus his partner and his secret heir. My mother would take the heat of the court battle with Warneke's children; allegations of undue influence, the insistent scrutiny of probate lawyers, would be too risky for Rittenhaus. And my mother could be trusted, afterward, to turn the house over to him; she would do it with dewy-eyed respect for a radical cult hero.

Julian Warneke had restored some of what he had taken from Rittenhaus. Apparently, it wasn't enough.

Apparently Manuel Boyd was right: Martin Rittenhaus had resented his role as Julian's cat's-paw, the night of March nineteenth. He'd resented Julian's cavalier and impractical scheme; resented sacrificing sixteen years of achievement so his partner could indulge in vicarious grandstanding.

For that, I couldn't blame Rittenhaus.

But poor Bess Warneke—sitting in Julian's office claiming to know some secret that would invalidate his will. Rittenhaus must have overheard her talking to Edward Hershey. Surgelato had snidely suggested that her murderer had entered the office with a key. I'd said no, we'd all liked Bess, all of us in the firm. And that was true. Felix Flish *had* liked Bess, I think. But what interpretation would he have placed on her words? Bess was a friend of my mother's; he'd wonder if Mother had confided in her.

After sixteen years on the "most wanted" list, paranoia would have become second nature. No use waiting to find out what Bess had discovered; waiting could be dangerous.

And then I had interviewed Rittenhaus's former secretary, Gayle Halberstam; met with the maker of *The Night of March Nineteenth*; and asked Karen Weillar's housemate about Rittenhaus. (Weillar must have told Rittenhaus or someone who knew him. My mother?)

Worst of all, I had heard Felix Flish slip up: I'd heard him recount an anecdote about a wino being thrown out of his law school.

According to the diploma over Felix's desk, he'd gone to Stanford Law. I'd never seen a wino on Stanford's campus (aside from frat boys): the surrounding neighborhoods were too exclusive. But I'd seen plenty of winos drift through Malhousie Law School.

Martin Rittenhaus had gone to Malhousie.

Rittenhaus had once been shaggy and bearded, with a small nose and thick glasses. He must have wondered: Had I seen past the rebuilt nose, the contact lenses, and the haircut?

Framing me for murder, as a last resort, might have been part of the original plan, but I hadn't been arrested yet, and I'd begun focusing police attention on Rittenhaus. Blowing me away has probably crossed many minds, and Martin Rittenhaus had better reason than most.

I crept into Felix Flish's office and stood there a few moments, staring at his diploma.

Stanford Law. Who would look for a runaway radical in that bastion of conservatism?

A Socialist Workers Party speaker had once given us tips on going underground: Find yourself a dead baby, he'd advised, someone born within a few years of you. Get a copy of his birth certificate, and use it to establish a paper identity. A Social Security card first, then a driver's license, then a high school equivalency diploma, then some college. College transcripts lend "checkability" to one's identity, he'd explained. So—if one becomes sufficiently desperate—does military service.

It must have taken Martin Rittenhaus years to make his identity "checkable" enough for Stanford Law. But it had been worth the toil: the diploma made him unassailably Felix Flish. It equipped him to resume his former life.

I turned away from the framed square of parchment.

Wasn't this what I'd wanted? To learn the truth before Edward Hershey, before Don Surgelato? To prove I was the clever one. The new, improved Nancy Drew?

And big joke: if I told anyone what I'd discovered, my mother's involvement with Rittenhaus would be revealed.

Not that Mother would be ashamed to have the world learn she'd conspired with a fugitive from justice. On the contrary: she'd be proud of her part in The Struggle. She'd insist on prosecution to the full extent of the law. No deals for my mother; it was the *symbolism* of the thing.

The full extent of the law. Mother had known Rittenhaus's identity and whereabouts, and she'd chosen not to reveal them. She could be charged as an accessory to his crimes.

Oh, it would pain her to learn her hero had murdered people, and nice, left-wing people at that. But Mother's sympathies were easily engaged. In mitigation, she'd consider Rittenhaus's years of hiding and suffering. And when it came to her part in helping him, in helping Karen Weillar, in helping god knows how many other underground characters, Mother would stand on principle. She'd use her trial as a forum; she'd quote Sojourner Truth until the judge had her hauled away for contempt.

Yes, I was clever (no one else would say it, so I might as well). I was so clever that if I didn't go to the police immediately, Felix Flish would kill me. I was so clever that if I *did* go to the police, my mother would probably end up with more jail time than the law school murderer.

• CHAPTER THIRTY-EIGHT •

I turned out all the lights, including the one in the reception area. I was on my way out to hail a cab I'd seen from Felix's window. I wasn't sure where I meant to go, but the wisdom of going had finally become apparent to me.

Too late, as it happened. I was reaching for the doorknob when I heard the tapping metal sound of a key missing its keyhole. I stopped, felt like my blood was draining away. I opened my eyes wider, as if that would help me see in the dark. But I heard the doorknob turn; I didn't see it.

I dashed back through the reception area, into our corridor of offices. I watched a shaft of light widen on the reception area carpet. An elongated shadow glided across it: Felix Flish. With a quiet click, he closed the door. The light vanished.

I flattened myself against the wall. I heard breathing; it wasn't mine.

Then I heard footsteps on the carpet. No lights; he hadn't turned on the lights. A bad sign. I groped along the wall until my hand encountered the knob of Julian Warneke's door. I prayed for oiled hinges and backed in, closing the door behind me.

The office was chill, emptied of everything but a bare desk and the shadow-boxed pastels of Mexican peasants. Headlights from the parking garage across the street made the room flicker with dim, uneven light.

He'd come looking for me. He hadn't turned on the lights, so he must be looking for me. He'd check every office; he might be reaching for Julian's doorknob right now.

I ran past Julian's photograph wall (Rittenhaus! Julian had taken down his pictures of Rittenhaus when Felix joined the firm!). The door to Julian's private bathroom was ajar. I went inside, closed the door, and depressed the lock.

The tiny room was dark, but not completely. A small opaque window let in a bit of light from the street. I could see myself as a dark shape in Julian's mirror, I could see my shoulders heaving with fear.

And I heard footsteps in Julian's office. I remembered my kitchen door, the six-inch hole blasted out of it. I forced myself to move away from the bathroom door, toward the window. With shaking fingers, with my head turned toward the door, I wound the crank that opened the window. Its squeaking seemed the loudest sound I'd ever heard.

Until I heard the bathroom doorknob turn.

I stopped worrying about noise. I clambered onto the toilet seat and stuck my head out the window.

There was a ledge out there, almost broad enough to walk along.

Twenty feet above the sidewalk.

I engaged in some wishful thinking; maybe I was wrong, maybe it wasn't Felix Flish in Julian's office. Maybe it was the janitor. Maybe it was the police. I'd nearly decided to warble, "Who is it?" when I heard a sliding thump. It was a sound I heard a dozen times a day. It was the sound of a desk drawer slamming shut.

Bess Warneke had come out of Julian's bathroom and dropped a key into his desk drawer: his bathroom key, I realized. A janitor wouldn't need Julian's key; he'd use a master. And a policeman would announce himself.

I went out the window headfirst, keeping my hands inside until my feet were firmly planted on the ledge. Then I pushed the window closed, shifting so my body wasn't silhouetted against it.

A freezing wind whipped my hair into my eyes, flayed it against my cheeks. My sleeve, torn from climbing into Mr. Cardoni's yard, caught the wind like a parachute. My blouse billowed with cold air. I looked down, saw someone climbing into the cab I'd meant to hail way down there. I forced my eyes back up, watched a car drive slowly through the parking garage across the street. How much noise had I made?

I heard the bathroom door open; I heard someone moving around.

Maybe Felix would think the police had left the door locked after Bess's murder. If I were quiet enough, maybe he'd go away.

I thought I heard the window open. I remembered my kitchen door, visualized my flesh exploding, the impact hurling me off the ledge. I waited for the shot, chest aching.

I waited there, just waited. The wind whistled in my ears, I could hear nothing else.

And nothing happened. I waited until I was so cold I thought I'd rather die than stand there any longer.

I edged back to the window. With numb fingers I discovered a gap between the window and the frame; thank god I hadn't slammed it tight. I wedged my fingertips into the crack and pulled until my fingers bled. It finally opened, and I slid inside as quietly as I could manage.

The bathroom door was wide open, but I was alone. I cranked the window shut and did some serious shivering.

I went out to Julian's office. That door stood open, too. I stayed close to the wall, edging toward it, listening for sounds. I'd almost reached it, almost convinced myself Felix had gone, when light flooded the corridor, spilling into Julian's office.

I flattened myself against the wall. It was Felix's office light. He'd apparently concluded his search and decided to stay a while.

I was too startled by that realization to pay heed to the sound emanating from the lobby. But Felix Flish heard it. He walked by Julian's door. If he'd turned his head he'd have seen me cowering there.

He was in his usual rolled-up shirt-sleeves and stockinged feet. It shocked me to see him looking so ordinary, so like the Felix I'd always known.

I heard a woman's voice; Felix had opened the door to someone.

The voice said, "Feeelix!" Matthilde Warneke. "I tried your house! I'm so glad I found you."

There was a pause, some throaty sounds. Kissing.

Felix murmured something. They passed Julian's door. Felix's arm was around Matthilde's shoulders. Her long hair fell over her cheeks like a nun's headdress.

"What's the matter, my beauty?" I heard Felix ask her.

"That contract you gave me, of Julian's—"

"Did you throw it away?"

"No, I—" Hesitantly, "I showed it to Willa."

"Willa! I told you to throw it away!"

"But you wanted me to tell the police, Felix! Isn't that why you showed it to me?"

Silence.

"And Willa knows that lieutenant. I hate talking to him; he's so cold! And anyway— Felix, that's what I wanted to tell you: it's not real!"

Felix's voice grew tight. "What do you mean?"

"I phoned that detective, the one who was at the wake. Hershey. I gave it to him." A pause. "What's the matter, Felix?"

"Nothing. Come out to the lobby with me." His office light was extinguished. "What did the detective say?"

They passed Julian's door again. Felix wore his shoes now. He carried his jacket awkwardly draped over his arm.

Matthilde was talking. "The handwriting was Julian's but the paper is a Xerox copy, a color Xerox—"

"Maybe Julian made himself a copy."

"That's what the detective said. Only, Felix—!" They stood no more than ten yards from Julian's door, in the middle of the reception area. "Julian never called Clement 'Clem'! Nobody does. And I was thinking, maybe somebody whited out the real name and substituted—"

Trapped in a B movie. I wanted to shout, "Shut up, you stupid woman!"

Felix Flish, Clem Kerrey: same number of letters. Julian had wanted Felix out; maybe he'd discovered Felix's affair with Matthilde.

Changing his will would have been Julian's next step, more than likely.

"Feeelix!" Matthilde cried.

As I stood there impotently cursing the woman's stupidity, Felix Flish fired a shot. Shot his lover, just like that.

A moment later, the reception area lights went out.

I stood there in fibrillating disbelief. Just like that? Just like that, he'd shot Matthilde?

I watched him walk slowly back toward Julian's office. I tried to make myself flatter, smaller, quieter. He entered the office woodenly, walking right past me. He went into Julian's bathroom. I watched him wipe the gun with paper towels, I watched him crank open the window and set the gun on the ledge. I watched him crank the window shut and wipe the crank.

Then he walked back through Julian's office. A moment later I heard the reception room door open and close.

• CHAPTER THIRTY-NINE •

I didn't expect the police to find me so soon. I thought I'd have some time with my parents. I wasn't sure what I meant to do with the time; I just wanted it. But it turned out the lieutenant was sitting in an unmarked car in front of their house. I was reaching for the doorknob when he stepped up behind me and gripped my wrist.

He startled me so badly I half fainted against him. I could feel the tautness of his muscles through his clothes. I could smell his skin. I turned and wrapped my arms around his neck.

His head dropped, fit itself against my ear.

Then he reached for my wrists, breaking my embrace and stepping away from me. My parents' Panamanian flags cast a pinkish glow over the porch. In it, Don Surgelato looked almost handsome.

From his breast pocket, he pulled a folded sheet of paper. He said, "Willa June Jansson, I have here a warrant for your arrest. You have the right to remain silent. You have the right to an attorney of your own choosing. If you cannot afford—" He faltered, looking at me. "If you cannot afford an attorney, one will be appointed for you."

"I know my rights, Lieutenant. Don't bother."

A dozen times he'd faced me as a cop and tried to persuade me he was a friend. He made no pretense now, in his most official of capacities, but I couldn't seem to think of him as a cop.

He shook his head. "Off the record, Willa. I don't believe

it. The order came from upstairs. From the commissioner's office. That's why I didn't send out a team; I came alone because I wanted to tell you that."

He took my hands, turned them over. My fingertips were scraped and bloody from pulling open Julian's window. He stared at them. "We got a radio call about an hour ago." He spoke without inflection. "Someone in a parking garage dialed nine-eleven; said there was a jumper across the street—woman on the ledge of your office building. By the time the uniforms got there, there wasn't anybody outside. They decided to go in and take a look. They found a body in your reception room. Radioed us. Did a warm search. Found a gun on the ledge outside Warneke's bathroom." He continued to stare at my fingertips. "And blood on the window frame."

I pulled my hands away, curling the fingers. I could still see Matthilde Warneke's face. I'd bent over her to see if maybe—

"Please raise your arms above your head."

I did as the lieutenant asked.

He frowned at the ground, running his hands lightly over my body. Then he pulled me down my parents' stairs, to the unmarked car. He helped me into the back seat and slammed the door.

I slumped there, eyes closed. I could feel the car move. I didn't want to involve my mother, god knows. But I couldn't let Felix get away with it.

"If I told you the truth, would you help me, Don?"

He stopped the car and turned around in his seat, extending a hand to me. His eyes were bright. "We'd do *everything*—I swear it, Willa—everything we possibly could for you."

I took the hand he extended, clinging to it. "Not we. It has to be you. It has to be to Don Surgelato. Not the lieutenant of the homicide division. I can't talk to the cops. Not about this."

He tried to pull his hand away. "I'm a cop, first and always. Jesus Christ! Do you hear what you're asking me?"

"Yes." I sounded defeated, even to my own ears. For the first time in months, I craved tobacco.

"Listen. I can help you more as a cop—"

"No. If it comes to a trial—I don't know. God." I could almost smell the excrement odor of jail cell, the cabbage smell of dining hall, the rank soap of communal showers, the body odor and mildew of the day room; and I could almost hear the hornet's buzz of a sewing machine. "It's like this: I know who the murderer is, but he knows something—"

"We make deals all the time, Willa. Immunity from prosecution in exchange for information."

I shook my head. "In court today, that boy—I'd have given anything to make him register. I offered to defend him without charge if they ever reinstituted the draft. I begged him to let me cut a deal with the U.S. Attorney, a guilty plea in exchange for a recommendation of probation. But he insisted: no deals. It was a matter of principle with him."

"But you don't feel that way, do you?" His tone was anxious. "About deals?"

I looked out the car window. We were parked opposite the most photographed street sign in the city: the corner of Haight and Ashbury. Beneath it, a group of overfed teenagers in expensive clothes giggled, maybe looking for some of the things the district had once offered. They carried double-decker cones from Bud's Ice Cream.

"No, I don't feel that way," I admitted.

"So we're not talking about *your* principles."

"Such as they are. No."

He got out of the car, unlocked the back door, and slid in beside me. "Talk," he said.

I stared at him. Could I trust him?

He put his hand on my cheek. "Before I come to my senses, Willa."

Before I came to mine, I told him the story.

He kept his head bowed, occasionally patting his pockets for phantom cigarettes.

I concluded wearily, "When I realized it was Rittenhaus, I thought it was revenge. And I could understand that—after all, Julian had ruined his life. But when Felix killed Matthilde—" I forced myself to look out the passenger window at the upscale ice cream parlor, to stop visualizing Matthilde's torso splattered over the reception room rug.

"It was business," Don said quietly.

"Yes. Julian was pauperizing the firm, exercising his control to freeze retainer fees. That was bad enough. Then he tried to buy Felix out of his early partnership. I've heard Felix talk about the firm, about controlling it—turning it around financially. It was important to Felix to make the business work, to make it his very own."

The lieutenant shifted his elbows to his knees, his forehead to the heels of his hands. "He could have killed you."

"I'd been to see Kit Kline. I'd connected Kline to Rittenhaus, and by extension, Rittenhaus to our Teamsters clients."

"And Kline was still loyal to Rittenhaus—to Flish."

"Yes. Local 16 is our firm's biggest account, and Felix planned to make it our most profitable one by drafting a new retainer agreement. If Jim Zissner had won Local 16's election, he'd have taken the local's business to another firm. That would have kept our firm—Felix's firm—in the red."

Surgelato raised his head. "So Flish either forced Zissner's car off a cliff or traded on his left-wing hero status to get Kline to do it."

"I think Kline has a lot of respect for the radical underground." I decided not to mention Kline's wife. "And I don't think he has much respect for the union. I think he purposely blew the election by acting crazy at the joint council." I could feel my shoulder muscles knot. "Mae Siegel—our secretary, Zissner's girlfriend—she didn't believe in Jim's 'accident.' She was going around saying it was murder." The knots grew painfully tight. "I guess Felix asked Kline to shut her up."

"Secretaries are in a position to overhear a lot of incriminating things their bosses say," Surgelato added quietly. "Flish had a lot to be nervous about."

A lot to be nervous about. I'd told Surgelato about the secret trust. I'd given him reason enough to get back behind the wheel, drive to my parents' house, and arrest my mother.

We stared at one another, the knowledge a barrier between us.

He said, "Do what I tell you. Exactly what I tell you." He breathed heavily. "It'll be tricky."

"What do you want me to do?"

"Go on record. Everything except your mother. Everything about Flish. All of it." His fingers dug into my shoulders. "You've got a bullet hole in your door? You can back this up? You're sure?"

"Of course I'm sure! But Don, you arrest him and my mother will come forward of her own accord. To show solidarity." I'd been a fool. Implicating my own mother.

"Not if things go right." He slid his arm around me. "Your law school murderer will be walking the streets in seven or eight years. We can't let Flish get away with murder, too. You understand that? Even if there's some risk to both of us."

"But my mother—"

"I'll take care of it." He kissed me. Arrested me and kissed me; I remember thinking it was almost kinky.

Then he climbed back into the front seat and drove me to the Hall of Justice. We didn't speak on the way.

• CHAPTER FORTY •

Activity ceased as Surgelato led me through the big room with all the desks. No one spoke. Everyone watched. I was conscious of my torn sleeve, the stains on my clothes, the wild state of my hair.

I tried to keep the faith, tried to trust the lieutenant.

He said to Inspector Krisbaum, "Get the waivers, Danny."

Krisbaum looked surprised. He pulled some papers out of his desk and followed us into the tiny cork-walled interrogation room.

To me the lieutenant said, "Please read this carefully, Miss Jansson. It states that you have been informed of your right to remain silent and your right to have an attorney present and that, having these rights in mind, you wish to talk to us now."

I took Krisbaum's pen and signed the paper. Krisbaum snatched it up as if it were a check made out to him.

"Will you also consent to having this session recorded on an audio recorder?"

I looked at him, alarmed. What if Krisbaum asked me about Julian's will? What if something slipped out about my mother?

But Don Surgelato nodded, almost imperceptibly.

"All right," I agreed.

Krisbaum slapped another waiver onto the table, and another inspector set a cassette tape recorder beside it.

Cassettes. That's what had startled me, at the end of *The Night of March Nineteenth*! That muted thumping sound: it was Rittenhaus, cracking his big toe in time to the music, just as Felix Flish had when he'd driven me to Julian's wake.

I began by saying, "I realized tonight that Felix Flish is really Martin Rittenhaus."

Krisbaum's face lit up like a Christmas tree. He glanced at the lieutenant.

And Don Surgelato quietly left the room.

• CHAPTER FORTY-ONE •

It took me about an hour. I went through it more or less chronologically: Felix Flish cracking his toe to a Rolling Stones tape, Matthilde Warneke showing me the dissolution of partnership agreement, Jim Zissner's death and Mae Siegel's certainty that it had been murder, the incident with Kline at the Teamsters' council, talking to Gayle Halberstam, watching *The Night of March Nineteenth* and seeing Kline with Rittenhaus, Felix's anecdote about Malhousie, my confrontation with Kline, being shot at in my apartment, and realizing as I walked the streets afterward that Flish had to be Rittenhaus.

"He'd seen me talking to Gayle Halberstam, he'd slipped up with that anecdote about a wino at his law school, and then I went and asked Kit Kline about him." I stopped. I could feel sweat soaking my blouse. What if Kline implicated my mother in retaliation for my fingering Felix? Jesus, what had I let Surgelato talk me into?

Krisbaum handed me a glass of water. I drank it. "I didn't want to go home; I didn't think it was safe."

Krisbaum had been joined by a dapper young man he'd introduced as Kelly. Kelly asked me, "Why didn't you call us?"

"I was in shock. I wanted to go someplace familiar, someplace where I could think about things. So I went to my office. It was stupid; I realize that. But I saw the streetcar, and I got on it. I was standing in the reception room when I heard footsteps. I got scared. I hid in Julian's office."

174

The rest of my story came haltingly. I began to cry when I told them about Matthilde.

After a while they turned off the tape recorder.

Someone tapped at the door. There was a furor outside; I could hear the raised voices when Krisbaum opened the door. I could see a crowd of detectives gathered, could hear one of them order a newsman to turn off his camera. Kelly offered me a fresh handkerchief while Krisbaum stepped outside.

A few minutes later, Krisbaum came back in, saying, "I hope you'll bear with us for a while, Miss Jansson. It's very possible the charges against you will be dropped, but we'll need to talk to you some more. It seems," he passed a hand over his flushed face, "it seems that Felix Flish attacked the lieutenant, trying to escape."

"Attacked!" I stared at him.

"Flish is dead." He sounded as surprised as I felt.

Behind me, Inspector Kelly exclaimed, "Holy shit!"

And to him Krisbaum remarked, "His first shoot! Flish musta gone bananas!"

• CHAPTER FORTY-TWO •

I was in custody overnight. It took that long for my story to be checked out and charges to be dropped.

I asked Krisbaum, "Didn't you ever take Felix Flish's fingerprints?"

"We had Flish's prints on file; got 'em from the bar association, in fact. But we didn't have Martin Rittenhaus's prints—nobody did. People used to be paranoid about getting fingerprinted back then. Rittenhaus never gave a thumbprint to the driver's license people, and he never gave prints to the bar association. He showed a bunch of other IDs, apparently, and made a big stink. Some fucking—pardon me—some committee of lawyers finally said, okay, he could practice law anyway. So sure, we checked Flish's prints." He tucked in a shirttail that a fellow inspector pointed to in passing. "Funny he gave his prints to the bar committee this time around. Times have changed, I guess."

I only saw Don Surgelato once. He looked harried. Krisbaum was with him.

"Well, Miss Jansson, looks like you were right about Flish."

"What happened, Lieutenant?"

He smiled bitterly. "You'll be reading about it in the papers."

I put my hand on his sleeve. "Lieutenant—"

I glanced at Krisbaum; I could feel the inspector hanging on my words. So I couldn't say the words I wanted to say.

With Felix Flish dead, my mother would have no reason to come forward and incriminate herself: what would be the point of showing solidarity with a dead man? And though Kit Kline would be questioned by the police, he wouldn't know I'd set in motion the chain of events that had led to Felix's death. He'd have no reason to implicate my mother.

All I could say was, "*Please* don't regret it."

Surgelato shrugged a little, turning away.

"His first shoot," Krisbaum told me quietly, as the lieutenant walked away. "But hell, what was he supposed to do, let Rittenhaus get away again?"

"How did it happen?"

"Lieutenant found him at home. Told him he was wanted for questioning. I guess the guy flipped. Lieutenant didn't say too much about it, but knowing him— He's not the kind of guy to blow somebody away without a hell of a good reason. Now your radical types, they'll be screaming 'an unarmed man!' But hell, if you knew Don like we do—" Hands curling into plump fists, Krisbaum squared off against a horde of invisible defamers. "Like the song says, 'To know him is to love him.'"

• CHAPTER FORTY-THREE •

Clement Kerrey drove me home. I'd thought of him snidely, doubting the sincerity of his smiles and his sentiments; and now I was ashamed of myself for it.

With two of his law partners dead and his life's work all but destroyed by bad publicity, Clement had taken it upon himself to comfort my parents—and to keep them away from the media circus at the Hall of Justice. He had waited for me himself, hour after hour on a fourth floor bench.

"I saw you come out of Mae Siegel's room," I admitted, settling into his car.

Muscles in his face twitched. He didn't speak until he'd mastered them. "I saw her walking through the casino the night before. I phoned downstairs and got her room number. I was going to"—the muscles twitched again—"fire her. Before the meeting with Local 92. Her door was unlocked. When she didn't answer, I went in. I spent about ten minutes doing CPR, but it was hopeless, I could see that. I called the desk and went down to deal with Local 92." He glanced at me a little guiltily. "Maybe that seems cold. I just felt"—he shrugged—"like Hank needed me."

"You didn't tell the police you'd found Mae."

"I did. When I called them. I told them they could find me in conference room three. Didn't they mention it?"

"No."

"I guess they wouldn't. It can't be in their best interest to get too chummy with people in an investigation like this one."

• CHAPTER FORTY-FOUR •

"**A**n unarmed man!" my mother exclaimed through damp Kleenex. "There's no excuse for what Martin did, but dear god!" She crossed herself. "To shoot him like a dog in the street!"

I was hiding out at my parents' flat. My place was a zoo: reporters at the door, constant phone calls.

"I was there when he killed Matthilde, Mother. He did it like you'd step on an ant."

"I'm not defending him! But he had a right to a fair trial, Baby! That lieutenant—"

"No!" I stood up, glowering at her.

Daddy came up behind me, putting his arm around me. "I think we'd better shelve this topic."

"You saw Mother with Julian, didn't you, Daddy? That's who you thought she was having an affair with."

My father winced; I'd betrayed his confidence.

Mother emerged from behind her Kleenex. "An *affair*?"

"Julian had arranged a secret trust, Daddy. Mother was the named beneficiary of his house. She was supposed to deal with all the lawsuits, and then when the place was officially hers, she was supposed to turn it over to Felix Flish."

Mother stood up, too, yoga straight and dignified. "I'm not ashamed of agreeing to do it. I didn't know that Felix would kill—" She pressed a wad of tissue to her mouth.

My father's forehead crinkled in astonishment; I was right—he hadn't known about the trust.

179

"Julian was thinking about changing his will again, Daddy. He was having second thoughts about leaving the house to Felix—I think he'd found out about Felix and Matthilde. That's why he was meeting Mother."

"I told him even if he didn't want to help Martin—" The tissue fell from her fingers. "There was Karen Weillar, wasting her life in an office— And— Oh, poor Julian!"

"A secret trust." I could see my father psychosynthesizing. "Then, if Flish hadn't died—if he'd been arrested, your mother—"

I nodded.

He looked at me, aghast. "You didn't have a hand in it, Willa?"

"I had to ask for help, Daddy. It was risky, but—"

"What was?" my mother wondered. "What are you two talking about?"

My father put out a hand to steady himself on the couch.

I changed the subject. "I'll have to find another job. The law firm's defunct. Clement's talking about teaching at Malhousie."

The phone rang. I went into the hall to answer it. It was Edward Hershey.

"Still want to know who wrote you those hate letters?"

"Is it anyone I know?"

"Yup."

"Will it depress me to find out who?"

"Don't think so. Not at all." His tone was cheerful. "Now, I can't prove it a hundred percent. It's not like I have photographs of the perpetrator in the act. But I'd be willing to testify for you, if it came to a lawsuit."

"A lawsuit? Who is it?"

"This is from comparing type of paper, print font, daisy wheel. Paper is the kind they use over at the federal building. Daisy wheel is a new little guy. Unique to a new model of memory typewriter. I got a list from the manufacturer of every

Californian who's sent in a warranty card for that model. Eighteen people in San Francisco. For all I know, every one of them hates you. But only one of them went to Malhousie Law School. Many moons ago, but he went there."

"Who?"

"The Honorable Manolo M. Rondi, U.S. District Court Judge, Northern District of California."

Rondi! I thought of the hatred he'd poured into those letters. We'd offended him deeply, Julian Warneke and I; until that moment I hadn't realized how deeply. We'd cut him to the political quick with our antiestablishment defenses, and apparently I'd come to symbolize something the old reactionary despised.

Well, I'd use that hatred against him, now. I'd threaten to sue him, threaten to move for a mistrial in the selective service registration case.

And maybe under the circumstances, Judge Rondi would find it in his heart to give the boy a suspended sentence.

"Edward," I said, "all is forgiven!"

ABOUT THE AUTHOR

LIA MATERA is a lawyer. She lives in Santa Cruz, California. She is the author of *Where Lawyers Fear to Tread* and the forthcoming *The Smart Money* and *Hidden Agenda*.

Special Offer
Buy a Bantam Book
for only 50¢.

Now you can have Bantam's catalog filled with hundreds of titles plus take advantage of our unique and exciting bonus book offer. A special offer which gives you the opportunity to purchase a Bantam book for only 50¢. Here's how!

By ordering any five books at the regular price per order, you can also choose any other single book listed (up to a $5.95 value) for just 50¢. Some restrictions do apply, but for further details why not send for Bantam's catalog of titles today!

Just send us your name and address and we will send you a catalog!